MY COUSIN KRISSY

Books in the Mackenzie Prentice Mysteries Series

October Fire

Buried in Treasure

Painted Lady

On the Edge

Old Habits

My Cousin Krissy

Mack On Ice (2026)

MY COUSIN KRISSY

A MACKENZIE PRENTICE MYSTERY

MARY PIERCE

ISBN: 979-8-9881776-1-6
Published by Seven Windows LLC

Book design and editing by Michelle Rayburn (missionandmedia.com)

Cover art by Mary Pierce

First edition 2026

To all who don't quite fit the mold
Who dance to the beat of those other drummers
Who've been called quirky, weird, or crazy
Who've been told they're too much or not enough

Here's to us!

I tell you, in this world, being a little
crazy helps to keep you sane.

—Zsa Zsa Gabor

CHAPTER ONE

Friday, November 21

MY MOTHER WARNED ME when I was just a kid. "Stay away from your cousin Krissy. Wherever she is, there's trouble."

I should have listened.

I hadn't seen my older cousin Kristen for almost twenty years. She'd graduated from Three Rivers High a couple years before me and then high-tailed it out of town.

But there she was at Old Town Tap on Friday night, the week before Thanksgiving. I'd stopped there for burgers with my friends—yoga-guru Tansy and artist Jade.

Krissy was at the bar trading shots with two guys I didn't recognize. I wouldn't have known it was Krissy, but I recognized her laugh—that high-pitched snort-laughing that Krissy always did.

Krissy is, um, what's the best word? Raucous? Loud? Outrageous? She was always "Crazy Krissy" growing up. ADHD up the wazoo, off-the-charts hyperactive. Super quirky.

"That's just Kris," Gram would say when she heard that Krissy had fallen off a garage roof trying to retrieve her Frisbee. She spent the rest of that summer with casts on both arms.

"That's just Kris," again, when she burned the garage down trying to make her own fireworks. It took months for her bangs to grow back.

"That's just Kris," after she went into the feral cat domestication business and ended up with rabies shots.

All that before the end of middle school.

So here she was at the Tap, Friday night, snort-laughing and chugging shots with two guys who looked like bikers. Serious bikers. And Krissy was keeping up with them shot for shot. Maybe she'd become a motorcycle mama in her years away.

Krissy is about five-ten and had always been athletic. She and her dad used to shoot hoops at the park across the street from their house. In high school, she played basketball and tennis and had that female-jock look, lean and muscular, in athletic clothes and running shoes most of the time.

She looked very different now. Rail thin, she was dressed in black leggings above black combat boots. She'd layered an oversized red-and-black plaid flannel over a black tee shirt. On the tee, snakes slithered from the eye sockets of a gray skull. Her hair, cut super short, was bleached white with green and blue streaks. As an adult, the true rebel was alive and well and dressing the part.

Rebel. Troublemaker. I'd been drawn to all that as a kid, though I'd mostly steered clear per my mother's orders. My anxious mother was anxious enough without any of her five children getting into trouble.

Compared to Krissy, I'm pretty bland. A just-right, Goldilocks kind of girl, according to my grandmother. Not too tall, not too short. "Just right," Gram says.

Just so-so, I say.

I overheard Krissy tell the two guys, and probably everybody else at the Tap, that she needed to "hit the head." She spotted me on her way to the restroom and came to the booth.

"Cousin Mack!" She punched me in the shoulder.

I stood and returned the punch with, "Crazy Krissy!"

She gave a snort-laugh and bear-hugged me, lifting me off my feet and shaking me.

I squeaked out, "G-good to see-ee you."

She set me down, and I caught my breath, then introduced her to Jade and Tansy. Kris reached across the booth, grabbed Tansy's hand, and shook her whole arm. Hard. Tansy winced. Jade's turn. Another wince.

"Join us," Jade said, massaging her fingers.

Krissy glanced at the two guys, gave them a wave, and hollered, "Later!" One of them waved back, and they left the Tap.

I gave her a quizzical look. "Friends of yours?"

"That's Slade and Jacko. Met them earlier outside the Kwik Stop. I told them I was coming to the Tap, and I offered to buy them a drink."

That's just Kris, picking up strange men at the convenience store and becoming instant friends.

I'd never seen them before. "Are they locals?"

"Nah, they're just passing through. And speaking of passing, I'll be right back." She headed to the restroom.

Tansy leaned out of the booth, watching Krissy. Jade looked at me, eyebrows up.

I gave a shrug and explained. "My cousin. Haven't seen her in years."

Tansy leaned back. "I think I remember her from school. A couple years older than us? Kind of wild, right?"

"Understatement," I said.

Krissy came back to the booth and ordered me to "Skooch over." I did, and she sat next to me. "Oof! Feels good to sit my ass down."

My bacon cheeseburger and fries arrived, along with Jade's veggie burger and Tansy's bunless burger with a side salad. My friends encourage me, gently, to take better care of myself, but my desire—some might call it addiction—for fat, salt, and sugar wins out every time.

Kris swiped half my fries, and I gave her half my burger. The four of us made small talk for another fifteen minutes while Tansy and Jade finished eating. Then Tansy said, "We'll let you two catch up." She and Jade left.

Krissy moved to sit across from me in the booth. I ordered a refill of my Diet Coke, and Kris ordered a beer. After the waiter left, she grinned at me and said, "It's been a long time, cuz. Look at you. You're all grown up, Dork!"

I smiled. "Nobody's called me that since you left. How's life been treating you?"

She snorted. "Life's effed me over, that's what. Until recently, that is."

"The last I heard, you were living up north."

"I was, but then I moved. And moved again. I like to keep moving." She'd lived north and south, east and west, but all within the state.

"We thought you might be dead."

She snorted a laugh. "Why would you think that, Dork? I stay in touch with my mom." Krissy's mother is my mother's youngest sister, Fiona, the youngest of Gram's six children, and the least involved with the family. Fiona's drinking problem has gotten worse over the years. Gram, my mom, and Fiona's other siblings have tried to talk to her. But Aunt Fiona is wrapped in a very cozy blanket of denial. Eventually a family gives up trying to help.

I said, "So what brings you back to Three Rivers?"

Kris got serious. "My mom's gotten herself into something and told me she needs help."

My investigator ears perked up. "*Into* something? What *kind* of something?"

"I'm not sure. She wouldn't tell me over the phone. She said *they* might be listening."

"Who are *they*?"

Krissy shrugged. "Who knows? She's getting a little paranoid, I think. It's all the booze for all these years."

In the past, Aunt Fiona has had what she calls her "spells." A few years ago, Fiona called my mother in the middle of the night, telling her that there were people outside in her yard. My mother felt a moment of panic until Fiona said they were dancing naked around her plum tree. Fiona was hallucinating. My mother told her to go to bed, sleep it off, and call her in the morning.

I reminded Krissy of that incident.

She said, "Yeah, we thought it was funny at the time, but looking back, it was probably a sign of what was to come. You can't drink like she drinks without losing brain cells. Her brain cells have probably been diving out her ears for decades."

"So she might be imagining things now, or she might be in real trouble? What kind? Financial trouble? Someone making threats?"

Kris shrugged. "Like I said, she didn't want to tell me over the phone."

"You'll be staying with her?"

"Yeah, but it's not the best. She's got a little bit of a mess at her house, but I can probably find a spot on the couch. If I can find the couch that is." She snort-laughed again.

"What about your old room?" I remembered Krissy's bedroom from sleepovers when we were kids. She had a huge collection of stuffed animals. And parts of real animals. A squirrel skull. Snake skins. Empty turtle shells. And an almost complete cat skeleton that she'd glued back together and hung from a lampshade. She'd glued marbles in the eye sockets. I woke up during a sleepover to use the bathroom, and as I was coming back to bed, the hall light glinted off those marbles. I swear that cat was watching me.

Krissy said, "I'm sure my mother has filled my room with her stuff. Last time I was there, it was already pretty full. I couldn't even see my old bed."

When people say they have a "little bit of a mess," you can be sure the mess is big. We all knew there was a "little problem with clutter" at Fiona's small house on the east side of Three Rivers. But not being able to find the bed? That's clutter on a whole different level.

Kris took a sip of her beer. "I worry about sleeping on that couch. There could be cooties in there."

I gave a shiver, grateful that we kids never had to worry about that kind of mess growing up. My mother was too anxious to allow cooties to infest our home. And we spent a lot of time at Gram's, where life is always clean and orderly. That could be where Little-Bit-of-OCD Me was born. Along with my sugar addiction.

I asked, "You think your mom is a hoarder?"

Kris shrugged. "Probably. I've seen those shows on TV. I think she spends a lot of time drunk-shopping, buying stuff on those hokey TV shows. And on Amazon." She drained the last of her beer. "My mom said something about you being a detective. Are you really?"

I took out one of my TriMak business cards and slid it across the table.

She read aloud. "TriMak Investigations. Whoa. Legit. Seriously legit!" She leaned back in the booth and flashed me a wide smile. "This is so cool, Dork!"

I gave a little shrug. "It's all right, I guess." *Modest to the core.*

Krissy tucked the card into her shirt pocket. "So if my mom needs some, uh, detecting, could you help? You know, for family?"

Oh crap. Another family freebie job for TriMak? Another pro bono case would not make my partners, Trip Kipling and Chief Bronson, happy.

But family is family, and Gram would tell me, "We do for family. That's just how it is." And if Gram said I should do this pro bono "for family," I'd have no choice. Because when Gram tells you to do something, you just do it.

I said, "You asking as a favor, or do you want to hire me?"

She sat back. "Oh, I can definitely pay you. Definitely! How much do you charge?"

I held up a hand. "Hold your horses. I need to know what's going on with Fiona first, before I know if I can even help."

"Fair enough," Kris said. "When she tells me, I can tell you."

We spent the next half hour reminiscing about our childhood antics. My older sister, serious, studious Stephanie, was too uptight, too structured, too focused to have much time for Krissy. And my jock older brother, Greg, was only interested in sports.

So Krissy and I used to hang out. We'd walk the neighborhoods as kids. She'd look for discarded cigarette butts to smoke, and I thought that was so cool, though I was never brave enough to try smoking one myself.

She gave a chuckle and said, "Remember that night we got so sick?" We'd had a sleepover at her house, ate popcorn and a whole bag of marshmallows, and drank a jug of red Kool-Aid. We both ended up puking all that up in the middle of the night, all over the living room Hide-a-Bed and the carpeting. She smiled. "Good times, eh?"

I wrinkled up my nose. "Your mom was, um, less than pleased." Fiona had gone ballistic.

Kris made a face. "Yeah. She made me clean all that up after you went home."

"Sorry about that. I would have stayed to help."

"She wouldn't have let you. Mom was pretty strict. Dad could be, too, but not like she was."

I said, "Your dad was such a nice man." Fiona's husband, Andy, was one of my favorite uncles.

"Yeah, he was pretty cool. When my mom was raging drunk, he and I would go down to the park and shoot hoops. Or go for a run. Until he had that heart attack."

He'd died halfway through Krissy's senior year of high school. Kris said, "After Dad died, my mom got really depressed, and her drinking got way worse. And since then, it's been drinking and spending and who knows what else she's got going on now."

The waiter came to the table, and Krissy ordered a bacon cheeseburger, a double order of fries, another beer, and another Coke refill for me.

While we waited for the food, I said. "Earlier you said life had effed you over, until recently. What's that about?"

"Buckle up, cousin," Krissy said. "It's been a bumpy ride."

CHAPTER TWO

KRISSY SPUN A LONG tale of lost jobs, false starts on various careers, and trouble with ex-boyfriends. "I get bored easily, with jobs, with men," she said. Over the past year, she'd finally found some semblance of peace living in Lost Creek, a little town an hour east of Three Rivers, on the way to the larger city of Delport, in Lakeland County.

"I've been working odd jobs outside Delport. Dog walking, gardening, house cleaning. Even seasonal work on some farms around there. Making just enough to get by. There's really nothing in Lost Creek. Just a café and the feed store, a gas station, and a bakery. But there is a casino. I'd go there after I got paid. First it was slots, then I got into blackjack. This dealer, Jared, taught me the game. I loved it."

She bit into the cheeseburger, wiped a dribble of grease off her chin, and continued. "One day, I started winning. That pile of chips in front of me just kept getting bigger and bigger. I figured I couldn't lose. So, I pushed all my chips in. And I won.

And I won again. And again. What a rush that was, winning like that!"

She took a swig of beer, set the glass on the table, then met my eyes. "I won big." She stopped talking and stared off into space, smiling.

I ate a fry while I waited for the details. None came. I finally asked, "How big exactly?"

She grinned. "Eighty grand worth of big."

I sat back. "Holy crap!"

"I know, right? I went to cash in. I couldn't wait to see the look on my friend Charlene's face. She's the cashier at the casino, but she'd taken a break. This kid who usually cleans up around the place was filling in. I gave him my chips, and he brought out the biggest pile of twenties—all bundled like you see at the bank. A huge pile." She gestured with her hands on the table. "Huge. Never saw anything like it in my life."

"I can't imagine," I said, and took a couple more fries.

She went on. "Anyway, I told him—Robert is his name—I told Robert I needed a bag to carry the money in. He took a Walmart bag from under the counter and started putting the bundles into it." She mimed the process. "But that bag ripped. I told Robert it wasn't going to work, trying to put all that money in a plastic bag. So he goes in the back room and comes out with this burlap sack from Longacre Feed and Seed. Longacre is the farm supply store just outside of Lost Creek, and you see those sacks everywhere. People use them for crafts and then sell the crafts. My friend Charlene makes these adorable little pumpkins from burlap. She sells them this time of year. And for Christmas, she makes Christmas stockings and tree skirts. And she makes placemats—"

I grabbed her arm. "Krissy! Focus! Tell me about the money in the sack."

She chuckled. "Okay, sorry. You know I get distracted." She pointed toward the lights above the bar. "Look! Squirrel!"

We both laughed. That's just Kris.

She went on. "Anyway, Robert stuffed all the money in that sack and handed it to me. You'd think it would be heavy, but it felt like I was carrying a sack of flour. Just bulkier." She gestured with her hands again, showing me what it was like.

I said, "Eighty grand is a lot of money. You know, you could put the money to work for you. My sister Stephanie is an investment adviser in The City. You could earn some serious coin off eighty grand."

She shook her head. "No, no, no. No investments, no banks for me. I live off the grid. Working for cash. Making enough to get by. The IRS doesn't need to know anything about me, my income, and for sure not this money. So mum's the word, okay?" She leaned toward me, lowering her voice. "And just FYI, this casino? It's not exactly legal."

She told me the casino operates from an old barn outside Lost Creek. In our state, only native tribes are allowed to operate casinos, on tribal land. She said, "The local cops look the other way. I'm sure the guy who runs it pays them off and has been doing it for years."

"Kris, you can't keep that money. It's from an illegal operation."

She gave me an intense look. "Who's going to tell? The people at the casino? Fat chance. Nobody else knows about this but me—" She paused, and the look got more intense. "And now you."

Did I imagine a threat in her tone? I didn't know what to say. I couldn't promise to keep quiet. I'd only recently gotten my investigator's license and didn't want to lose it. Words like "aiding and abetting" and "accomplice after the fact" and "obstruction of justice" floated through my mind. But I took a deep breath and pushed all that aside for the moment because I wasn't a hundred percent sure what I should do. And besides, well, Krissy is family.

I held up my right hand and said, "Okay. For now." I hoped she wasn't going to ask me to cross my heart or pinky swear. She didn't. I asked, "Where's the money now?"

She finished her beer and leaned in again. "It's locked in the trunk of the car. I left Lost Creek in a hurry. The morning after I won the money, Jared, the dealer, texted me." She brought up the text and held the cell so I could read the screen.

He says we cheated! RUN!

She laid the phone back on the table. "I texted him back but got no answer. So I ran. I packed my clothes, took the money, and got the heck out of Dodge."

I asked, "Who did he mean? Who said you cheated?"

She gave a shrug. "Probably the guy who runs the place. Marcus Grubb."

I had to ask the hard question. "Did you cheat, Krissy?" Even as I said that, Rational Me wondered, *What difference does that make if the place is illegal to begin with?*

She leaned back in the booth as she laid both palms firmly on the tabletop. "Absolutely not. I might be kind of loose with my scruples, but I'm not a cheater. I'd never try to cheat, not even in that casino."

I said, "Okay, I believe you. But this guy, Marcus, is accusing you and the dealer of cheating. Did you notice anyone following you to Three Rivers?"

She lowered her voice. “Here’s the thing. I was afraid of exactly that, so outside Lost Creek, I stopped at this garage run by my friend Charlene’s ex brother-in-law, a guy named Delroy Bean.”

I chuckled. “Delroy Bean? Marcus Grubb? Where did these people get these names?”

Kris said, “I know, right? It’s almost like some weirdo made them up, huh? And Charlene was married to Delroy’s brother, Darrell. So she’s Charlene Bean.”

My turn to snort. “I would have kept my maiden name.”

Krissy shook her head. “No, her maiden name was something like Krakawojakowski. Not sure how to spell that. She kept the married name even after the divorce. I can understand her wanting to keep it simple, even if Charlene Bean sounds a little goofy.”

Kris polished off her burger and continued. “So anyway, Delroy agreed to take my car in exchange for another one. Rules about registrations and license plates don’t matter a whole lot to Delroy when he’s helping a friend. Or in my case, a friend of an ex-sister-in-law. And he was very interested in the wad of cash I handed to him. He gave me this old car and agreed to hide my car for me until I can figure out what to do. He’s got an acre of junkers behind his garage. I swapped my car for his and drove here.”

I used the last french fry to wipe the plate clean of the remaining salt and ketchup. “Can you trust this Delroy?”

“Sure. Charlene told me he’s a good guy. Of course, like most of us, he’s been in trouble. I remember hearing about this one time—”

I cut her off. “So this car that you got from Delroy is sitting outside right now? With eighty thousand dollars in the trunk?”

She shushed me and nodded.

I pushed the plate away and wiped my mouth on my napkin. "Maybe we should get out of here and get you to your mother's. You can hide the cash there."

We stood, and I reached for the check. Krissy grabbed it first. "I've got this, cuz."

I protested. "But that check includes what my friends ate too."

Krissy pushed my hand away. "My treat. I insist!" She pulled a wad of cash from the pocket of her plaid shirt and tucked several crisp twenties under her beer glass on the table.

I thanked her, and as we headed outside, I said, "Come over to Gram's tomorrow, okay? I'm sure she'd love to see you. And she makes cinnamon rolls on Saturday mornings."

Krissy grinned. "Mmm. I remember those."

"See you tomorrow then. And Kris, it's great to have you back home."

She said, "Not sure how long it'll be, but I'm here for now." She pointed to a car in the lot. "That's my ride."

The decades-old Oldsmobile Cutlass Supreme had more rust than paint on its long front end, home to a roaring V8 once upon a time. The faint remains of an ancient shine on those fenders hinted at the pride of the owners who'd once driven this marvel of American manufacturing know-how. The good old days.

As we walked toward the Olds, Krissy sucked in a breath. "What the hell?" she yelled and ran to the car. I followed her.

The passenger side window was smashed, and the passenger door hung open.

CHAPTER THREE

"WHAT THE HELL?" KRISSY hollered again as she looked into the car. "No! No! No! Somebody took my suitcase!" She looked around.

Why do we look around like that? Do we think whoever took our stuff is waiting to see our reaction to the fact that they took our stuff? I tried to be reasonable. "Okay, okay. So you can get some new clothes."

The look Krissy gave me told me that she wasn't interested in reasonable. "You don't get it, Mack! I had money in there. Lots of money."

"*All* the money?" For a second, I thought it would be a relief if somebody had stolen all of Krissy's ill-gotten gains.

"No, not all of it. But about twenty grand. The rest is in the—oh no, no, no!" She ran around to the driver's side door and pressed the trunk release, then ran to the trunk and opened it. "Oh, thank God! It's still here!"

I joined her. A burlap sack sat in the middle of the trunk.

She held it open, and I looked inside. Money. Bundles of twenty-dollar bills. Lots of bundles.

I said, "Well, this is good. At least they missed taking this, huh?" Looking on the bright side is one of the dumb things I do sometimes.

She glared at me. "Yeah, but I need to find the bastard who took my suitcase." She clenched her fists.

Rational Me couldn't resist saying, "You have enough money here to replace whatever they took."

She looked away, swallowing hard. "Stop, Mack. You don't understand." She looked at me, tears welling, then slumped against the side of the car. "That suitcase was special." She described a dark blue, hard-sided Samsonite case with wheels. Small enough for a carry-on, big enough to hold what you need for a weekend trip. "I took it when I left home at eighteen. My mom was so mad. She said it was the one nice thing she'd ever owned. Got it for a wedding present when she married my dad. It had a sticker on it from Hawaii, from their honeymoon." She frowned. "The more she demanded I give it back, the more I wanted to keep it." Her voice went soft. "She cared more about the damn suitcase than about the fact that I, her only daughter, had left home." She swallowed hard as she looked away, wiping a hand across her face.

After a moment, she took a deep breath, let it out, and looked at me. "When I left home after high school, I didn't just take the suitcase. I took a ring and a watch from my mother's jewelry box. I figured if I needed money, I could hock them." She looked down at the ground. "I never told my mother that I took those things. She thought she misplaced them. I need to go back to my apartment and get the jewelry. Then I'm going to just sneak it back into the house. She has so much crap around, she'll never notice. I'll never have to confess."

"But confession is good for the soul, Kris." *Geez, you sound like a nun! Butt out!* Obviously, my recent stint with the sisters of Holy Assumption Convent had had an influence.

Kris raised her brows. "When did you get so holy?"

I shrugged. "Okay, so tell your mother you took the jewelry, or don't. Up to you."

"If I tell her now, she'll go off on one of her rants, and I'll have to hear about it for days. You know what kind of temper my mother has."

I nodded, remembering one Easter Sunday at Gram's when I was a kid, back when Fiona and the rest of my aunts and uncles would gather at Gram's for holidays. Back before Papa Powell died.

My mother said something to Krissy's mother—one of those big-sister-to-little-sister things—and Fiona flew into a rage and started to throw a piece of ham at my mother.

Gram grabbed Fiona's arm just before she released the pork projectile, saying, "No quarrels, especially not on Easter Sunday. Now you two girls shake hands."

My mother had extended her hand, and Fiona stared at it, then finally, limply, shook it. Dinner continued, but I never forgot that flash of anger, the violent impulse I'd seen in my aunt that day. And Krissy no doubt saw that far, far more often.

I suddenly felt even more sorry for Kris. I put a hand on her arm. "Kris, I understand why you don't want to say anything about the ring and the watch. I'd feel the same way if Fiona was my mother."

She smiled and nodded. "You get it. I knew you would." She leaned against the back fender, pulled a pack of Camels and a Bic lighter from her shirt pocket, and lit up.

Rational Me went into detective mode. *Investigate the crime scene. Would they have left fingerprints opening the car door? Maybe. But a bazillion hands have touched this old car over the years.*

I checked the back seat. An old newspaper on the floor. Cat hair. Maybe dog hair. Maybe human hair. A greasy ceramic mug from a café somewhere. A paper cup and dirty napkins. No telling how long those things had been in the car.

No buttons that just happened to fall off the thief's coat. You only see that stuff on TV. This was real life, where clues are hard to come by, not conveniently left behind so the crime can be solved in under an hour.

I backed my way out of the car and stood next to my cousin.

Krissy gave a sigh, letting out a cloud of smoke. "I'll bet Jacko and Slade took my suitcase." She smacked a palm to her forehead. "Stupid! Stupid! How could I be so dumb?"

I patted her shoulder. "Don't beat yourself up. We can't be sure it was them. Anybody walking through this lot might have noticed the suitcase and taken it. You can't be sure."

She shook her head. "Well, then I was an idiot for leaving it there in plain sight. But hey, I thought, *It's Three Rivers. What could happen?"* She met my eyes, looking disappointed. Disillusioned. "The town has changed since I've been away, huh?"

I agreed. It did seem that, lately, more bad stuff was happening in Three Rivers than when we were kids. And working for TriMak, I spent my days dealing with lost things and lost people. Selfish people who don't think twice about taking things that aren't theirs. Cruel people, leaving broken hearts in their wake.

"The town has grown, Krissy. And bad stuff happens here, just like everywhere else. People are people. It's still nothing like what happens in big cities. It's still a pretty great place to live."

She let out a long sigh. "I'll agree with you after we get my suitcase back." She took another drag, held the smoke, then exhaled it in a cloud.

I didn't want to tell her how unlikely it was that we'd find her stuff. Whoever took it had likely opened the suitcase, taken the money, and then tossed the case and her clothes into the nearest dumpster.

I walked to the trunk, and Kris followed. "Since you can't lock the car now, let's secure this money better until we can get it to your mom's house. I'll tuck the bag behind this other stuff." I moved a cardboard case of empty beer bottles and another grimy box of old auto parts. I grabbed the corner of a grease-stained quilted pad—one of those gray blankets the moving people wrap your furniture in—and pulled it. Under the furniture pad, I saw another burlap bag with Longacre Feed and Seed printed on it.

"What's this?" I pulled the second bag toward me.

Kris shrugged. "No idea. That's not mine."

I pulled the bag forward into the light from the parking lot.

She said, "Do you think whoever took my suitcase left this?"

"Not likely. This has probably been in the trunk the whole time since you traded cars with that Delroy guy."

She pulled the sack open and looked inside. "What the—?" She held it toward me. "Look!"

I peeked in.

Bones. Lots of bones. I took hold of the sack and started to pour the contents onto the trunk floor. Little bones and bigger bones clattered into a pile.

Back in school, studying the bones of the body was particularly fascinating for me. For a while, I imagined everyone I looked at as a skeleton, picturing what they looked like under the skin.

Every gender, race, and creed—all the same, under the skin.

I started to tick off the names of bones I remembered. "Phalanges, tarsals, femur, ulna, radius, clavicle." Not that I could have told you which bones were which.

Krissy grabbed my forearm. "It's an animal, right? Please tell me this is an animal!" She looked at me, wide-eyed.

The last bone rolled out of the bag.

A human skull. That one I recognized for sure.

The skull rolled forward, revealing a big hole in the back of it. Then it wobbled back and finally settled on top of the other bones.

Looking at us.

I sensed Krissy trembling beside me. Her voice went squeaky. She made a little strangled sound as she asked, "Is that what I think it is?"

I nodded. "It's not a what, Krissy. It's a who. A whole lot of pieces of who."

CHAPTER FOUR

WE STOOD IN SILENCE for a long minute. Then Krissy hissed, "What the frick am I supposed to do with this? With him? Or her?" She pounded a fist on the back fender of the Oldsmobile, repeating, "What the frick? What the frickety frick!" She reached into the trunk and grabbed the skull. "I'm puttin' all this back in the bag, and then I'm tossin' it off a cliff somewhere!"

I grabbed her arm. "Stop, Krissy! Don't touch the bones!"

She stopped and looked at me, her eyes huge. "Oh crap. Now my fingerprints are all over his head. Now what the frick are we going to do?"

It was "we" now. "Well, for now, *I* will put the bones back in the bag." I pulled my hands up into my sweatshirt sleeves—my go-to technique to avoid leaving fingerprints—and put the bones back in the burlap sack. I was especially careful to wipe the sides of the skull to remove traces of Krissy.

With the bones hidden behind the furniture pad, I let out

a sigh as I closed the trunk. "There. Now *we* are going to leave whoever this is right here, and *we* are going to think."

Side by side, we leaned against the trunk lid. She took out another Camel and extended the pack toward me. "Want one?"

I shook my head. "That was your dad's brand, wasn't it?"

She nodded. "Yep. Right up until his heart attack."

"He was a good guy," I said.

"Yeah, he was." She took a drag and let it out, then looked at me. "When did you quit smoking?"

I said, "I never smoked. Not even those gutter butts you used to pick up. Never smoked. Never will."

She gave a shrug as she lit up. "Suit yourself." She sucked on the Camel, letting the smoke drift out of her mouth and up into her nose.

I crossed my arms and stared into the Tap's parking lot. We said nothing for several minutes. One of the overhead lights flickered and made a loud buzzing sound.

I said, "They need to replace that bulb."

"Yeah," Krissy said.

"Nice night," I said. This is evidently the kind of casual conversation people have after they've discovered a dead person.

"Yeah, nice night," said Krissy.

"Might snow soon," I said.

"Hope not," Krissy said.

Snarky said, *Great conversation. You're brilliant, Sherlock.*

"Kris, do you think this Delroy Bean would kill somebody and put the bones in the trunk of a car on his own lot?"

"He is kind of a doofus. Anything is possible."

I said, "Maybe the bones were in the trunk when Delroy got the car. He might have had this car sitting there for ages, planning to use it for parts. Never even looked in the trunk."

Krissy finished her cigarette and ground the butt into the

pavement with the toe of her boot. "Well, Detective Prentice. What do we do now?"

I stepped away from the car. "I'll probably have to go to Lost Creek and see this Delroy guy, find out what he knows about these bones. Meanwhile, for tonight, you go to your mom's. Put that bag of cash and the bones somewhere safe. Don't say anything about the bones. More importantly, don't *do* anything with the bones. And you might want to get this, uh, vehicle off the street just in case somebody followed you to Three Rivers."

She nodded. "I'll park it in my mom's garage and drive her car while I'm in town."

"Great. And I'll check with the chief about what to do next." I was pretty sure he'd tell us to turn the bones over to law enforcement. And not spend the money from the casino. The chief was deer hunting out of town. I texted him and got a canned reply:

Out of town. Back Monday

I said, "Until I can talk to the chief, do not—and I can't emphasize this enough, Kris—do *not* under *any* circumstances touch those bones. Got it?"

She gave a shrug. "Yeah, yeah, yeah. Don't touch the bones. Got it."

"Come to Gram's in the morning, and we'll figure out what's next."

She agreed and got into the Olds. After a long grinding, it started. As she put it in gear, it gave two loud pops, then belched a black cloud of smoke as she rumbled off.

This was going to be interesting. Time with Krissy always was.

I'd warned her not to touch the bones.

She'd promised not to touch the bones.

As she drove away, I was pretty sure she was gonna touch the bones.

That's just Kris.

CHAPTER FIVE

Saturday morning, November 22

I WAS SOUND ASLEEP ON Saturday morning in my loft bedroom in the carriage house behind Gram's Victorian. Chloe, my cat, snoozed at my side.

I was dreaming that I was lost in The City—what we call the metropolis a couple hours from Three Rivers—trying to find my way home. This is a recurring dream of mine, and sometimes I can make myself fly in my dream, above the trees and the buildings. Flying dreams are my favorite kind, and there I was, aloft, floating along, looking down on places that looked like places I've been before but don't remember. The sound of banging on the carriage house door broke the spell. I woke up pissed.

Through the fog of angry semi-consciousness, I heard Krissy yelling, "Mackenzie! Get your ass out of bed and open this door, you lazy slug!"

Chloe jumped up and ran downstairs. I swung out of bed

and pulled a hoodie on over my pj's. I headed downstairs as Kris pounded, yelling, "It's your ever-lovin' cousin! Open up, Dork!"

I opened the door and scowled at her. "Quiet down." I looked at the kitchen clock. "It's not even six yet. What are you so amped about?"

"My mom and I sat up all night talking."

I knew Aunt Fiona to be quite the chatterbox when she'd been drinking. Which meant she was quite the chatterbox most of the time, unless she was asleep.

Krissy, still in her clothes from the previous night since her suitcase had been stolen, clomped in and sprawled across a chair at my kitchen table. "You got any coffee?"

"Gram will have coffee on." I looked out the window toward Gram's. Her kitchen light was on. "I'll get dressed, and we can go over there."

Krissy followed me back upstairs to the loft. I quickly pulled the bedsheets and the duvet into place.

Kris chuckled. "You always made your bed. I remember that from your house growing up. You guys always had to make your beds."

"Yep, my mom had a few rules. Not too many, but they were enforced. Make your bed. Hang up your clothes. Don't leave wet towels on the bathroom floor."

Krissy said, "Boy, there was nothing like that at my house. Chaos reigned. If I wanted clean clothes, I had to do the laundry. Lucky if the sheets got changed twice a year. My dad did his best, but my mother didn't care." She wrinkled up her nose. "Which makes it even more ridiculous that she went on a rant this morning about the quote-unquote mess I'm making in her living room. My God, Mack. You can't even see her floor. I cleared the crap off the couch to make a tiny space for myself to sleep. She's freaking out about my moving her stuff. She said, and I quote, 'I won't be able to find anything!' As if you can find anything in that pile of crap she's got."

I'd been in a hoarded house before, but that one had things more or less neatly arranged in bins and boxes. Fiona's house sounded like one of those hazardous, toxic-waste-dump hoards you see on TV. Who knows what lurks in a mess like that?

Krissy went on. "She cares more about all her crap than she does about her own daughter! Jesus!"

I went to my closet and changed into my jeans, a long-sleeved tee, and a sweatshirt. "Did your mom give you any details about the trouble she's having?"

"Oh, yeah. Big trouble. Money trouble. Credit card debt from all the shopping. She did one of those payday loan deals that racks up interest by the minute. She can't pay them, and she's got other bill collectors after her too. She might even have put her house up as collateral. She's not a hundred percent sure."

"Anybody actually threatening her physically?"

"Not yet. Phone calls and letters from credit card companies. Somebody showed up at the house twice, and bill collectors even talked to her neighbors."

"There are rules about that stuff." I knew from past cases about the Federal Trade Commission's debt collection laws. "But if they don't actually threaten her, it's not illegal." I pictured some big guy with a broken nose threatening to break little Aunt Fiona's kneecaps. "Poor Fiona. She must be frantic."

Krissy gave a snort. "'*Poor* Fiona'? My mom? Are you kidding? She met the last guy at the back door with a meat cleaver and told him she'd bury him in the backyard if he came back. He told her he was going to report *her* to the police for threatening *him*. She's not 'poor Fiona.' She's a badass beyotch when she needs to be."

Ah, yes. Fiona's temper. "Has she called the police?"

"No. She doesn't trust them. Says they always took my dad's side when the neighbors called the cops about them fighting. She's hoping you can help."

"Okay. We can go talk to her later."

"No, she's going out of town with her friend Harold. Overnight." Krissy air quoted. "'To get away from all the stress,' she said."

I frowned. "So you come to town to help her, and she's leaving?"

Kris gave a shrug. "You got it. That's my mother."

I was filling Chloe's food and water dispensers when Krissy's cell phone rang. She looked at the screen. "It's Jared, the blackjack dealer."

She put the phone on speaker.

"Kris!" A male voice.

Kris said, "Hey Jared. What's up?"

A second of silence on the other end, then a streak of curse words the like of which I've never heard. He had to be making some of them up. "You better <&%#*> bring back the <&%#*>money or we're both <&%#*>! Understand?" He groaned. "Marcus wants it back. Kris, you gotta bring it back." He gave a little whimper. "You're not the one with your nuts in a vise here!"

Kris started to say, "But I don't have all—"

He cut her off with a shout. "Arggh! Just bring the money back! You clear?"

"Clear, Jared! I'll do my best."

He disconnected.

Anxious Me freaked out a little. *What if these nasty people are tracking Krissy's phone? Now they know exactly where she is, and we're all in danger.* I suggested that to Krissy.

She said, "This old phone? It barely makes calls and does texting. No camera. No GPS."

I looked at it. It was ancient, one of those limited-capability early cells. I let out a sigh, relieved. "Okay, I guess it's safe."

"Yeah, it's like I'm from a previous generation. Like an old lady."

I thought about Gram, who'd embraced her cell phone wholeheartedly when my brother Greg got it for her. Early on, I was a little annoyed by the number of times she texted me in a day, but that had settled down. Now it was just a text at night, what she called a "text tuck-in." Often she'd say, as she did when we were kids, "Sleep tight. Don't let the bed bugs bite." Or simplified in a text, "Sleep tight. No bugs. No bites." If and when I ever had a guy in my bed, how could I explain Gram interrupting whatever we might be doing with her text tuck-in?

Lonely Me doubted I'd ever have to worry about that.

We crossed the yard to Gram's back porch. The sun was just coming up. The early air was crispy cold. I took a deep breath and watched the fog of exhale.

Krissy shivered and hugged herself. "Colder than a witch's teat out here."

"You don't have a winter jacket?"

Kris said, "No, I left it behind in Lost Creek. Like I said, I have to get back there to get my stuff."

We took the steps up to Gram's back porch. Through the window in the door, I saw Gram in the kitchen, as expected, drizzling a spoonful of sugary glaze onto a pan of cinnamon rolls.

Kris hid behind me. I rapped on the window. Gram looked

up, smiled, and waved me inside.

I went in first. "Look who's come to visit," I said, and Krissy stepped around me.

"Oh, for heaven's sake! Kristen!" Gram set her spoon down and went up on her tiptoes to hug Krissy. "So good to see you, sweetie!" Gram held her at arm's length, appraising. "And you're too skinny. Sit. Sit. These rolls will be ready in a second."

We sat at Gram's round oak table. Kris smiled and inhaled deeply. "I remember this kitchen. Always smelled like cookies." She glanced at the cupboard. "You still have that big hen cookie jar. I love that thing!" She looked around. "And the rest of the flock."

Gram is chicken crazy. Salt and pepper, cream and sugar, napkin holder, and the clock on the wall—everything is poultry-themed.

Gram grinned. "My chickens are still here. That's how it is when you get older. Your own flock has flown the coop, and they need replacing." Gram got serious. "I'm sure your mother was delighted to see you. How is she doing?"

Krissy shrugged. "Same old, same old. Drinking too much and shopping too much. I'm here to help her get out from under it all."

Gram gave a sad smile, shaking her head. "It's kind of you to want to help, but will she actually let you? She's never been one to accept help from any of us."

Kris said, "She's a stubborn old lady, for sure."

Gram laughed. "If my daughter is an old lady, what does that make me?"

Krissy smiled. "Wise. Kind. Patient. And sweet. Best grandma ever."

Gram gave Krissy another hug around her shoulders. "I

know it wasn't easy for you, growing up in that house. I understand you staying away, and I'm glad you've come back to us."

"Not sure how long I'll be stickin' around, but it's great to see you again."

Twenty minutes later, I was just starting my third cinnamon roll when my mother and Duncan showed up. My mom had been living at Gram's, but she'd been staying at Duncan's pretty much full-time since they got engaged a few weeks ago.

This morning she looked perky in a pink sweatshirt with BRIDE written on the front. With her long brown hair in pigtails, she looked like a teenager. I couldn't remember the last time—if ever—that my mother looked this happy. And I was happy for her.

Duncan is good for my mother. He settles her, calms her anxiety, and she seems at peace when he's around. We all love Duncan.

Gram asked, "What are you two up to today?"

My mom said, "We want to go back and take another look at this wedding venue we found. It's in a renovated barn. We were out there last weekend and stopped at a little café. The owner of the café said they could cater our reception at the barn. But I don't know if we need a caterer."

Small family weddings in these parts are usually "catered" by family members.

Gram piped up. "You deserve the wedding of your dreams this time." My mother had married my father at the courthouse because she'd been expecting my sister Stephanie and didn't want a big fuss. I always wondered if they got married because they "had to," as people used to say. Maybe my father never really loved my mother, and that's why he walked out one night to get cigarettes and never came back.

That's probably why I have abandonment issues and probably why my mother has resisted getting into relationships. Until Duncan. There's just something about Duncan—his steadiness, commitment, reliability. Good old Duncan. Maybe she feels like she can relax and trust a man again.

I sincerely hope, in my heart of hearts, that Duncan is that man. And I equally sincerely, in my heart of hearts, hope I will someday have a Duncan of my own to trust.

I tuned back in to the conversation at the table. My mother said, "Lots of old barns in that area have been converted to event venues. Weddings, grad parties, retreats—all kinds of things like that."

Gram, who grew up on a farm, shook her head. "I can't imagine making an old barn pretty enough for that kind of thing."

Duncan said, "They put in new hardwood floors and good lighting. You don't feel like you're in a barn."

My mother said, "You wouldn't know it was a barn except for the shape and the openness. So it's a possibility for the wedding. Anyway, this little café had fabulous food. The best quiche I've ever tasted. Wasn't the quiche delicious, honey?"

She touched Duncan's arm, and he gave a murmured "um-hmm" through his mouthful of cinnamon roll.

She said, "We could serve that quiche at our reception, couldn't we, honey?"

He um-hmmed again, but his jaw tightened. *Trouble in paradise?*

I asked, "Did you like the quiche, too, Duncan?"

He swallowed hard. "I went for the sausage and egg on a biscuit. Tasted great." He looked at my mother. "I'm not a quiche kind of guy."

My mother's voice went flat. "I know that, honey." A moment of tension passed between them before my mother turned to the rest of us. "And here's something else. In the café, we overheard two men at the next table talking about an illegal casino operating out of a barn in that area. They said that the government—the *federal* government, like the FBI—is on to it. Isn't that something? Things like that just don't happen around here."

Krissy looked at me, wide-eyed. I gave a little shake of my head. She nodded. *Message received. Mum's the word.*

Besides, it would be rude to disrupt the Saturday morning cinnamon-roll-and-wedding chatter with, "Hey guys, Krissy won eighty grand illegally, maybe at that same casino. And also, we found the bones of a dead guy in a burlap sack. Anyone want to take a look?"

I sat back, thinking. The information traveling small-town grapevines often contains at least a kernel of truth. Likely it was the same casino. How many illegal casinos operating out of barns could there be in the area? I wondered if the chief had any federal contacts. You know how it is—you know somebody who knows somebody. I held my phone out of sight under Gram's table and sent another "need to talk" text. I got the same response.

Out of town. Back Monday

The conversation continued—the wedding, the weather, the upcoming holidays. Normal family stuff.

Nathan came downstairs eventually and joined us. He is Gram's third husband, in his eighties, and is, as he says, "losing it." He saw me and said, "Good morning, Evelyn." He sometimes thinks I'm his late wife. Gram corrected him and introduced Krissy.

I realized Krissy had never met Nathan, even though he and Gram have been married for over ten years. *How can that be? Families are supposed to stay together, aren't they?* But children grow up and move on. Just because I still lived in my grandmother's backyard and my mother had lived upstairs in the Victorian, and just because my brother Greg and his family lived practically around the corner, it didn't mean all families stayed close. My sister Stephanie lives two hours away in The City. And little sister Deanne lives a couple hours south with her husband and four kids. And brother Robbie lives in LA. Half of us are close and the other half not so much.

The fact is, regardless of our geographic locations, I rarely spend time with my siblings. All of us are busy with our own lives.

Lonely Me whispered, *It's just a fantasy that families stay together.*

I was glad Krissy was back. How long she'd stick around was uncertain, but for now, here she was.

CHAPTER SIX

IT WAS AFTER NINE Saturday morning. We'd eaten the last of Gram's cinnamon rolls when Krissy reminded me she needed to get some clothes. I suggested a trip to Target on the south side of town.

Three Rivers was all a-twitter when the Target store had opened a few years back. Our town isn't huge, but our central location makes us a shopping hub for this part of the state. There are lots of smaller towns around us, and people don't always want to drive the distance to The City to shop. So, Target saw an opportunity and graced our town with its presence.

Kris said, "Target's fine for undies, but who in town has the good stuff?" She tugged on the front of the black skull and snakes shirt.

Good stuff? More like weird stuff. Snarky can be really judgy.

Gram turned from the sink where she was washing the cinnamon roll pan. She said, "Go see my friend Lou Burgess. She'll hook you up."

I chuckled. "Did you just say 'hook you up,' Gram?"

She gave a sassy toss of her head. “I know what kids say these days. I’m with it.”

“You’re cool,” I said.

“Hip,” Gram said.

“Groovy,” I said. We could go on and on like that, Gram and I.

“Nifty,” said Gram.

“Far out,” said I.

“Stop,” said Krissy, in mock annoyance. She smiled, wistful. “I’ve missed you guys.”

Gram dried her hands on a dish towel, then grabbed Krissy’s hand. “Oh, sweetie, we’ve missed you too. I’m so glad you’ve come home.”

“Temporarily,” Kris said. “Just to help my mom out.” I waited to see if she’d tell Gram about Fiona’s troubles. Thankfully, she didn’t. Gram has enough worries.

Gram smiled. “We’ll take whatever time we have with you. We love you.”

Krissy stood, cleared her throat. “I better get rolling. Gotta get some clothes and other stuff.”

I asked Gram if Krissy could borrow a winter jacket. Gram brought her one that Nathan wasn’t using anymore. Brown suede with shearling lining, bomber jacket style.

Kris slipped it on and ran her hand along the suede front. “Whoa! This is so cool. So vintage!”

I stood. “Speaking of vintage, I’ll text Lou and see if she’ll meet us a little earlier at her store.” Lou opens her shop on River Street at ten on Saturdays. She texted back, saying she’d meet us at the store at 9:30.

With hugs all around and assurances from Gram that we didn’t need to stay to help her clean up, we left.

Outside, I noticed that Krissy had used duct tape and a

white garbage bag to cover the broken side window of the Oldsmobile. When she tried to start the car, it gave a few grinding sounds and died. Kris got out and thumped her fist on the roof. "Stupid frickin' piece of junk! Harold tinkered with it last night and said he'd fixed it. But obviously not." She kicked the driver's door, "Damn! How am I supposed to get around without a car?"

"I thought you were going to park this one in your mom's garage and borrow hers."

"Yeah, she hemmed and hawed, then finally admitted her car was repo'd. She's got a real mess, Mack. I want to use my money to help her out. Get her car back, or make sure she keeps her house."

I shook my head. "No, Kris, you can't spend that money. The casino is illegal, and you heard what my mother said. The casino might be part of a federal investigation. I have no idea why feds would be involved. If they even are. At the very least, that casino is violating state laws. Regardless, you cannot spend that money. Where is it, by the way?"

She looked forlorn. "I put the sack behind the furnace at my mom's. But I left the bag of bones right where you hid it last night." She opened the trunk. "See? The bones are right—" She sucked in a breath. "What the frick?"

I looked. The furniture pad had been moved. The bag of bones was gone. "Krissy, where are the bones?"

"I've got no frickin' clue."

I had to ask. "Kris, you said you were going to toss them somewhere. Did you?"

Left hand on her heart, right hand raised, she said, "No! Scout's honor! I put the sack of money behind the furnace at my mother's, but I left that bag of bones right where you put it."

"Then how are they gone now?"

She gave a little snort. "Duh! The car's not exactly secure with that busted window."

"You said Harold was working on the car. Could he have moved the bones?"

"Maybe, but he and my mother took off in his camper early this morning, remember? To get away from all the stress, she said. So typical. Make a mess and then take off, leaving someone else to clean it up!" She pounded a fist on the car again. "So typical! Arggh!"

"Call them and ask if they moved the bones."

Kris shook her head. "I can't. My mom doesn't have a cell, and if Harold does, I don't have his number." She started to hyperventilate.

I patted her on the back. "Okay, okay. Let's just take a breath. Calm down." I led her through a few cycles of breathing, just like Tansy taught me. "That's right . . . breathe in . . . breathe out . . . and again . . ."

After a few rounds of slow breaths, Krissy seemed calmer. I said, "Here's what we'll do. We'll get you some clothes at Lou's and Target. Then we'll go to your mother's place and look around. The bones must be there somewhere. Sound good?" I pointed at the junker. "That'd be a chilly ride, if you could even get it started. Let's take my car."

As we drove to Lou's, Jimbo chirped from under the back seat.

Krissy craned her neck to the back and said, "You've got a cricket in your car. You want me to stomp it?"

Jimbo went quiet. I swear he understands English.

"Absolutely not!" I explained how Jimbo came with the Ford Escape when I bought it from my brother Greg. Jimbo's presence is why I call the car Cricket.

Krissy rolled her eyes. "You were always a sucker for lost critters."

I huffed. "Excuse me? You were the one who got rabies when you decided to tame all the feral cats in the neighborhood."

She smiled. "Good times. Good times," she said softly.

CHAPTER SEVEN

LOU'S VINTAGE IS ON River Street in downtown Three Rivers, not far from the TriMak office. Just a few weeks ago, the street was decorated for Halloween, the lampposts and storefronts festooned with pumpkins, witches, black cats, and white ghosts.

The day after Halloween, all of that had been replaced with giant sparkling snowflakes and lights draped around the trees. Now, white twinkle lights created a sparkling tunnel over the street, and every store window was decked out for the holidays.

Krissy hummed "Jingle Bells" as I parked Cricket in the alley behind Lou's. Before we got out, I said, "We have to find those bones, Kris. There was a big hole in the back of that skull, right?"

"Yeah, right," Kris said. "Maybe they took a bad fall and died?"

"Or it could mean the person was murdered."

"Jesus! I want to think they just fell down."

I said, "Okay, but for the sake of argument, let's say it was murder. Then somebody had a very good reason to hide them. And we have a very good reason to find them and give them to the authorities." I didn't look forward to telling the chief we'd found bones and then lost them.

"I just want my suitcase and my money. I don't care about the bones."

As we got out of the car, questions tumbled through my mind. *Who took the suitcase? Who did the bones belong to? Where did they come from? Why were they in that trunk? Where were they now?* So many questions and absolutely no answers.

Lou was inside the back door of her store, inflating a four-foot-tall plastic blow-up turkey. She plugged the plastic cap into the turkey's air hole and set him on the floor. He swayed and then flopped over on his tail feathers.

"Who's your friend?" I asked.

Lou helped him stand up. "Promotional freebie. I'll set him out front, weighted down with a brick. Who's *your* friend?" She looked at Krissy and smiled.

I made the introductions and thanked Lou for opening the store early for us.

Kris told her, "Some jackwad stole my suitcase, so I have nothing but what I'm wearing. My gram says you can hook me up."

Lou chuckled and looked at me.

I nodded. "Yep, Lou, those were Gram's exact words. Hook her up."

Lou laughed. "Well, let's see what we can do."

What Krissy did was make a pile on the counter of pretty much every piece of black clothing Lou had in the shop. Two black camisoles, a black bustier with a lace-up front, and a pair of black jeans with a bunch of zippers along the right leg.

Standing at the counter—"in front of God and everybody," as Gram would say—Kris stripped down to her black sports bra. Then she put on a black tee shirt with the words I'M YOUR IDEA OF A GOOD TIME on the front and, on the back, THINK ABOUT IT. She topped that with a black-and-green buffalo plaid flannel in a men's XXL.

We were about to wrap things up when Krissy spotted something in the glass case where Lou displays vintage jewelry. "Can I see that one?" She pointed at a bracelet.

Lou slid the back of the case open and took the bracelet out, laying it on a piece of black velvet on top of the glass.

"Ooh. Check this out, Mack," Krissy said. The bracelet was actually five thin golden snake bangles with green stones for eyes. Each snake's mouth clasped its tail. Stacked together, they formed what looked like one continuous snake. "This is so cool," she said, her voice soft, almost reverent.

"It's very old," Lou said. "Probably around the time of Tutankhamun—"

Krissy blurted, "You mean King Tut? That's ancient."

Lou gave her an indulgent smile. "No, no, I mean around the time Tut's tomb was discovered in the 1920s. Snakes were a thing for those ancient Egyptians. And snake jewelry became popular around that time."

"How much do you want for it?" Krissy asked.

Lou said, "It's gold-plated, so ninety-five dollars?"

"I'll take it!" Krissy said.

Lou took a piece of tissue paper from under a counter and started to wrap the bracelets. Krissy stopped her and said, "I'll just wear them."

Lou rang up the total while Kris pushed up her sleeve and stacked the bracelets on her left arm. Then she reached into the pocket of her jeans and pulled out a twenty, a five, and two ones. She muttered, "Oh crap," and turned to me. "I'm tapped out, cuz. This is all I have."

She looked so sad that I couldn't help but offer to help. "No worries. Keep your cash, and I'll pay Lou. You can pay me back when—" I glanced at Lou. I didn't want to say anything more. Lou and Gram talk all the time, and I didn't need Gram asking me questions, or worse, getting involved in any investigation. I finished with, "When you can."

Krissy beamed as Lou bagged up the clothes. I paid Lou with my debit card, and thanked her for opening the store early for us.

"No problem." She smiled and winked. "Glad I could 'hook you up.'"

We left Lou chuckling.

Twenty minutes later, we walked into Target. Krissy continued repeating the mantra she'd started in the car. "Underwear, socks, and makeup. That's it. Underwear, socks, and makeup. That's it."

She'd said it about twenty times when I teased her, "So Kris, I'm starting to think maybe you need underwear, socks, and makeup. Is that right?"

She laughed. "If I don't say it over and over, I forget, and then I buy all kinds of other stuff. ADHD, you know?"

I laughed. "Oh, I know. I know." I have a touch of ADHD myself. Maybe it's genetic. Maybe my father had it. For sure, my creative brother Robbie does. And maybe brother Greg does, too, but he just channeled the energy into athletics. Not likely a problem for sister Stephanie, who was always goal-driven. And youngest sister Deanne is so busy with her four little ones, you can't tell if anything else is going on with her. All the commotion with four young children makes it hard to tell where motherhood ends and ADHD might begin.

An hour later, Krissy's cart held underwear, socks, and makeup. And three pairs of black jeans. And two pairs of black leggings. And four long-sleeved tees—two plain black ones, one in a camo print, and the fourth tee in acid green with OVER IT printed in white on the front. On top of all that, she'd added a pair of gray plaid pajamas and another pair—pink with little sheep bouncing around.

I shot her a quizzical look. "Pink? Sheep? Seriously?"

"I love pink, and who doesn't like sheep?" She smiled and then frowned, biting her lower lip. "Oh God, I forgot about Lambie Pie. She was in my suitcase. I've had her since I was a kid, and she's gone with me everywhere. You remember her?"

I nodded. Lambie Pie was one of the menagerie in Krissy's childhood room.

Kris squeezed her eyes shut. Tears leaked out anyway. My big, tough, crazy cousin—crying over a stuffed toy.

I patted her arm. "We'll find you another Lambie Pie. Don't worry."

She swiped at her cheeks as she rolled her eyes. "As if there's another one in the world like her!" She glared. "Those bastards! Keep the damn money, just give me my lamb!"

Krissy calmed down as we finished shopping. She was all set, and I was out just shy of three hundred dollars.

Back in Cricket, Krissy said, "I'll pay you back, I swear. All my money is in that burlap sack, and you're telling me I can't spend it. The rest was in the suitcase. I just kept out a few twenties. And I spent most of that at the Tap last night."

"What about your bank account, your ATM card?"

"I don't have a bank account. I, uh, run my life on cash," she said.

I wondered how anyone could function these days without a bank account. "When you worked, where did you deposit your paychecks?"

"I worked for cash. Dog walking, cleaning, gardening were all cash jobs. Always."

I said, "You don't pay taxes." A statement, not a question.

She shrugged. "Hey, I always just made enough to get by. Can't give the government what I don't have."

Living hand-to-mouth. No bank account, no savings, no retirement plan. I'd negotiated a good job at TriMak, with generous benefits. I'd gotten lucky. Who was I to judge my cousin?

"You can pay me back whenever," I said.

She thanked me.

As we left Target, Kris said, "All that shopping worked up an appetite. I'm starving. Where should we get lunch?"

I was still full from the cinnamon roll I had at Gram's. Snarky snarked. *Roll? You mean* rolls, *as in four. With butter. And that heavy whipping cream in your coffee.*

I checked the time. Eleven fifteen. "The Tap opened at eleven. You want a burger?"

"With bacon and cheese, yeah. Maybe some onion rings. And some cheese curds," she said. Food was obviously her comfort. Her broken-hearted-lost-my-lamb soother.

As she buckled herself in, she repeated a new mantra, "Bacon and cheese and onion rings, please. Bacon and cheese and onion rings, please. Bacon and cheese . . ." all the way to the Tap.

Annoying? Not. At. All.

That's just Kris.

CHAPTER EIGHT

WE DROVE NORTH ON Second Avenue toward Old Town Tap. As we passed the Northland Suites Motel, a red truck came out of the motel parking lot and whipped by, heading in the opposite direction.

Krissy yelled, "Hey! That's those two guys from last night. I remember that truck, and the driver is that Slade guy. Or maybe he's Jacko."

I whipped Cricket into an illegal mid-block U-turn and followed them. They stopped at the light on Second and Lake, and I tapped the horn. The driver looked into the rearview mirror, and the passenger craned his neck to look at us.

Krissy lowered Cricket's passenger side window and leaned out, waving and yelling, "Hey Slade! Jacko! I want to talk to you guys!"

The passenger—Slade, maybe—startled, evidently recognizing Krissy. He said something to the driver, whom I assumed was Jacko, and as soon as the light changed, they charged forward. Obviously not in the mood for a chat.

I followed, faster and faster. *Detective in hot pursuit.*

They continued south. "I'll bet they're heading for the highway. Hang on," I said.

Kris grabbed the handle above the side window as I took the turn fast.

They went faster, heading toward the business district on the south side of town.

Krissy jabbered, rapid-fire. "They wouldn't run if they weren't guilty, right? Right? They've got my suitcase! And the money! Go faster, Mack!"

I pushed Cricket as far as I dared. Faster than Gram drives, but significantly slower than the chief would. Jimbo chirped like crazy. He gets excited when I push the speed limit.

We closed in on the truck. I handed her my cell. "Take a picture of their license plate! Camera's on the home screen."

Krissy fumbled with the phone for what seemed like forever but finally snapped the photo. "Got it!"

The red truck reached the entrance to Milcross Builders. A semi-truck was blocking the right lane as it backed into the Milcross lot. I expected Slade and Jacko to stop, but they whipped around the front end of the semi, nearly hitting an oncoming car in the left lane. I slammed on the brakes.

You can never win a contest with an eighteen-wheeler.

The big truck finished backing in, and by the time the road was clear, the red pickup was nowhere in sight.

Krissy pounded the dashboard in front of her. "Damn! They're probably taking my money to Vegas!" She let loose a long burst of swear words as she continued pounding.

Jimbo and I went silent. We just let her vent.

I drove around the area, past the strip mall, through the parking lots, and along the frontage road. No sign of the red truck. I said, "They probably got on the highway, and we have no way of knowing if they went east or west. But we do have the license number, and maybe we can track them down."

Kris asked, "You mean like on TV, where you call your contact at the DMV?"

"I don't have a contact at the DMV."

"So then you call your cop-friend at the police department, and they agree to do it on the sly for you?"

I couldn't imagine Heather Sullivan being willing to help me like that—on the sly or not. And I wasn't asking any other officers I knew to risk their jobs for me. "Nope, sorry. But we've got something better than a friend at the DMV. We have the chief. Or we will when he gets home from hunting."

Krissy, calmer, looked at me. "Okay, meanwhile, what do we do, Detective?"

"We go back and talk to the people at the Northland Suites. Maybe those two said something about where they were headed."

Krissy gave me a salute. "Yes, ma'am! Let's do it. This is so exciting. I'm like your deputy or something." She pretended to pick up a mic from the dash, as if we were in a squad car. She pressed the fake mic key and made a squawking sound. "Dispatch, One-Adam-Twelve returning to motel to interrogate staff."

I shook my head. "You watch too many old TV shows."

"This isn't TV," she said. "This is the real deal, and it's exciting!"

She pretended to put the fake mic back and started beating out a rhythm on the dashboard with the "duh-duh-duh-duh-dahhh-dah" theme song from *Hawaii Five-0*. "Two-eleven in progress! Book 'em Dan-o!"

I didn't want to tell her she was mixing her TV show quotes. She was obviously having a good time, and I wanted to let her. She'd gone from angry to sad to happy and now goofy.

So Kris.

A YOUNG GUY NAMED DEVIN WAS behind the desk at the Northland Suites Motel. I handed him my card and lied my face off. "I'm assisting in a federal investigation."

Krissy stifled a snort and turned her back.

Devin's eyes got big. "Feds? Wow. How can I help you?"

I leaned toward him. "Two men left here half an hour ago. Red truck. What can you tell me about them?"

He looked at his computer screen, tapped the keyboard. "John Smith rented the room. Had a red truck. Stayed in room 106."

John Smith? Oh brother.

"How did he pay?"

"Cash. In advance." *No credit card record then.*

Krissy turned and glared at Devin. "Did they have a suitcase with them? Dark blue, with wheels and a sticker from Hawaii?" She pounded a fist on the counter. "And don't lie to me!"

Devin shrank away as I grabbed Krissy's arm and pulled her back. "Don't mind my partner, Devin. She's had a lot of caffeine today." I glared at her and motioned with my head for her to walk away. She took three steps back. I looked at the kid. "Did they have a suitcase?"

He cleared his throat, and his voice squeaked a little when he said, "No, ma'am, not that I noticed. They just had a duffel bag. Ma'am. Sir." He gave a worried glance in Krissy's direction, and she curled her lip at him. He turned back to me, eyes wide.

"Devin, this is very important. Did they say where they were heading?"

He shook his head. "No, but they seemed in a real good mood."

I said, "We'll need to see their room."

"I'll take you down there. Housekeeping hasn't started yet." He escorted us to room 106 and opened the door.

Motel Clerk Devin was cooperating superbly with Mackenzie Prentice, Federal Investigator. I said, "We'll take it from here."

He cleared his throat. "I'm not supposed to . . ."

I gave him my most serious look, brows knit and frowning as I lowered my voice. "That will be all. The government thanks you for your cooperation, Devin."

It's surprising how good I've gotten at lying. Occupational hazard.

He cleared his throat again and squeaked, "Just be sure to close the door when you leave."

After he was gone, Krissy said, "They're probably heading to Vegas. Or Atlantic City."

I reminded her, "We can't be sure those two took your suitcase with the money in it. It could have been somebody else."

"Why else would they have run from us?"

I said, "We don't have all the facts yet." I walked around the room, looking for anything that might tell us where Slade and Jacko were headed. Any indication that they'd taken Krissy's suitcase, or any connection between them and the casino. Anything at all.

Nothing. An empty bag from Burger Barn. Six empty beer cans on the dresser.

I checked the bathroom. Wet towels on the bathroom floor. *My mother would be appalled.* No toothpaste gobs left in the sink. *They probably don't brush their teeth. Disgusting.*

I came out of the bathroom. Krissy was sitting on the edge of the bed. She looked up, hopeful. "Anything?"

I shook my head. "No clue where they were headed. No sign of your stuff." We walked out of the room and shut the door behind us.

As I backed Cricket away from the building, a light rain started. With the temperature hovering around the freezing mark, we could have snow later. I turned the car around and headed toward the street.

Suddenly, Krissy slapped her palms against the dashboard and yelled, "Stop!"

I jammed Cricket's brakes. "What?"

She pointed into the bushes next to the lot, to our right. "My suitcase."

I put the car in park, and we got out and walked to the bushes. Krissy's suitcase lay upside down, with her socks, underwear, and makeup scattered under the shrubs. She turned the case over. She picked up a brown tee shirt from the ground and held it up for me to see.

On the shirt front was a picture of a white horse rearing up and the words FRISKY PONY. The horse and the words were bedazzled with sparkly beads. "My friend Charlene gave me this last Christmas. Now it's ruined." She pawed through the remaining clothing. "The money's not here."

I helped her gather the rest of her stuff and put it back in the suitcase. The hinges were bent, and the case wouldn't close, so she wrapped her arms around it and carried it to the back of Cricket. I raised the liftgate, and she set the case inside.

I was heading for the driver's seat when I heard Krissy's strangled cry. "Oh no! Oh no!"

I ran around the car. Kris looked stricken as she pointed to the ground. Two little pink fuzzy legs and a little tail stuck out from under Cricket's front tire.

"It's . . . Lambie," she said.

"Oh crap," I said. I got into the driver's seat and backed Cricket up. Krissy bent down and came back up holding the poor, dirty, soggy stuffed lamb. She hugged it and got into the car.

As we drove, she picked gravel out of Lambie Pie's face. "She's all in one piece, but poor Lambie. Poor Lambie." She kissed it.

I said, "Okay, now we know for sure that Jacko and Slade were the ones who took the suitcase. But why? Was it just a crime of convenience? They just happened to see it and decided to steal it? Did they know it was your car?"

She said, "Oh, yeah, they knew it was my car. They saw me at the Kwik Stop getting gas. They knew. They knew. They knew . . ."

She repeated that as she hugged the lamb all the way to Old Town Tap.

CHAPTER NINE

EVERYBODY IN THREE RIVERS knows that Old Town Tap has the best burgers. Other restaurants have tried to take the title, but the crown belongs to the Tap.

Krissy tucked Lambie into what was left of her suitcase in the back of the car, and we went inside. Vince Hampton was at a table with three other guys—his fellow firefighters. They were in sweats.

I'd had a crush on Vince, a friend of my older brother Greg's, since I was in middle school. We'd flirted lately but hadn't done more than that. He'd wanted to and I'd wanted to, just never at the same time.

Vince looked up, waved, and came over. He gave me a quick hug and a peck on the cheek. "We just got done with a training session. Came over for a late lunch."

I introduced Krissy to Vince. He took Krissy's hand to shake it.

She straightened up to her full five-ten and met his eyes. "Whoa. Dude," Krissy said softly.

Vince flashed her a grin—his grin full of mischief that is absolutely adorable. That grin he has when he knows he's getting to you. His dark eyes get even deeper when he does it, and I always feel kind of krinkly inside when he aims that look at me.

Krissy must have felt that way too. She whispered again, "Whoa. Dude."

I swear I saw a jolt of electricity pass between them. I expected one or both of them to catch fire any second.

"Buy you a beer," Vince said. Not really a question.

"Uh-huh," Krissy said, nodding.

Krissy struck dumb? Hard to imagine, but there it was, right in front of me, and if I weren't hoping to get something going with Nick Milcross, I'd have felt jealous.

To be honest, part of me did feel jealous in that moment, the part of me that said, *Wait! What? Both Vince and Nick are supposed to be mine. At least until I decide which one I really want.*

But that part is stupid and selfish, and Rational Me knows that a guy like Vince isn't going to be content with just one woman, even Fabulous Me. So I watched them walk away to the bar. They acted as if I'd disappeared. I was invisible. I'd ceased to exist, and it was just the two of them, setting off on an adventure together. A hot, sexy adventure.

I'd completely lost my appetite, and Lonely Me wanted to cry. Lonely Me wanted to text Nick and see if he wanted to get together. But I knew that would just be using him to make myself feel better.

I felt like Vince had just dumped me or something, which is stupid because we're not together. We're not dating. We'd gone out occasionally, but it's nothing exclusive, nothing serious. I'd made that clear to Vince, or maybe he'd made that clear to me. I was having trouble remembering at the moment because Vince and Krissy were at the bar, cozied up to each other, his hand—his hot hand—resting on her arm, and their foreheads almost touching.

I turned away. It was too painful to watch. I texted Jade and Tansy to see if either was free for lunch. I needed a friend.

Jade got to the Tap ten minutes later. I was standing by the door, nursing a Diet Coke. She took one look at me. "What's wrong?"

I gestured with my head in the direction of Krissy and Vince at the far end of the bar.

"Oh crap," she said. "Let's get you out of here. We'll go to Jimmy's."

Jimmy's Pizza has been in Three Rivers since the beginning of time. It's the place high school kids hang out. Back in high school, a bunch of us would pool our resources to come up with the five dollars we needed to buy one large pizza. And you had to eat fast if you wanted more than one piece. These days, Jimmy's small plain pizza costs fifteen dollars. Times have changed.

The windows at Jimmy's were fogged up, the air inside warm and smelling of spices and melted cheese. The hand-painted wall murals depicted scenes from Italy—gondolas in Venice and hills with white houses, overlooking the azure sea.

A big sign from the Three Rivers Chamber of Commerce congratulated Jimmy's on fifty years in business, next to photos along the wall of the original Jimmy—James Carducci and his wife Antoinette, side by side in white aprons, smiling at each other, working together. In love. Lonely Me sighed. *Will we ever have that?*

Jade and I took a high-backed booth along one long wall. She sat facing the front door, and I faced the rest of the dining room.

While we waited for our pizza—veggie on Jade's half and meat lovers on mine—I told her how I felt about Vince and Krissy. "I mean, Vince and I don't have anything official going on. Really. He's free to date or whatever with whoever, and it's really none of my business."

"Really." Her tone said she wasn't buying it.

I snarled. "Yes, really!"

"Then why did you call me?"

I looked at the table. "You know how it is. Even if you don't have anything official you still . . . you know?"

"Oh yeah. I know." The pizza came, and we dug in. Jade was just about to take another bite when she looked up and said, "Uh-oh."

"What?"

She focused on her pizza and said in a loud whisper, "Don't look!"

So of course, I turned around and looked.

Nick. Walking into Jimmy's with a girl who looked very familiar. I ducked my head and pretended to be looking for something under the booth.

After a moment, Jade hissed. "It's okay. They're gone. He didn't even look this way."

The girl was Hillary Sharp. I'd met her at Spider Spidowski's Halloween party the previous month. I was there with Nick. That night, Hillary was dressed like a slutty Little Bo Peep, and she was Spider's girlfriend. At least she had been then.

I moaned. "Ugh! This can't be happening! First Vince and now Nick. What are the odds this happens on the same day, within an hour?"

"It's crazy," she said.

I whined on. "My life is turning to crap. I'm living in a crappy soap opera! The last time Nick and I talked, I told him I wasn't ready for a commitment. He was asking for one, but I said I wasn't ready." I looked at the table, shaking my head. "I keep screwing things up. I'm such an idiot."

She grabbed my hand. "It's okay. *He's* the idiot. If he was so ready to commit to you, how does he jump to someone else that fast?"

"I don't blame him. I blame myself. He's a great guy, and now he's moved on. I blew it." I rubbed an imaginary spot off the tabletop with my index finger as I fought tears.

Lonely Me was heartbroken. *He doesn't love us anymore. That's why he hasn't called or texted or come by. He's moved on.*

Snarky wasn't as gentle. *You blew it, Sherlock. Nice going, stupid.*

Jade squeezed my hand. "Mack, I'm so sorry."

I scowled, pulled my hand free, and waved the waiter over. I wanted a drink. Nick had told me he was concerned about my drinking, and I'd quit three weeks ago. Not for him but for myself. Just to see how it felt to go without. Not that I have a problem. I'm not like my Aunt Fiona.

But at that moment, I wanted a drink. Any drink. A Bloody Mary with extra vodka sounded good. I started to say, "Bring me a blood—" and stopped.

Rational Me stopped, actually. *You don't want to do this. This is not the answer.* Every part of me knew that was the smart choice.

I pointed to my half-empty glass of Diet Coke. "Can I get a refill? And an order of cheesy bread? Please?"

I looked at Jade. She and Tansy had warned me before that I'd lose both guys if I didn't make up my mind about which one I wanted. "You and Tansy were right, Jade. Now Vince is with Krissy. And Nick is with Bo Peep. And I'm alone. That old song is my theme song now." I sang a little. "*Alone again, naturally . . .*"

Jade squeezed my hand, too good a friend to say she'd told me so. Instead, she said, "You're not alone. I'm here for you. Tansy and I are both here for you. Don't ever forget that."

I raised my glass in a toast. "Here's to Mackenzie Prentice, Man Repeller."

She raised her water glass and tapped it against mine. "To better days," she said.

"And better men," I added, then chugged the rest of my Coke.

CHAPTER TEN

JADE DROVE ME BACK to the Tap to get my car. I debated going inside to be sure Krissy had a way home. Badass Me snapped. *Don't be such a sap. Vince will be more than happy to haul her ass around.* Badass was right and grumbled all the way back to the carriage house.

Little-Bit-of-OCD Me knows just what to do when I'm upset. Since I'm not drowning my sorrows in alcohol anymore, I cleaned. Then I cleaned some more.

I cleaned all the rest of Saturday afternoon. I scrubbed and scoured every crack and crevice of the carriage house, including every slat of my blinds. Mirrors. Counters. Light switches.

I stripped my bed and washed the bedding—blankets included—in the stackable units in the main floor bathroom closet. Nick had installed the washer and dryer during the carriage house renovation. *Such a handy, helpful guy. Where is he now? Having a great time with Bo Peep, no doubt.*

Rational Me said, *You don't know that for sure.* But I was pretty sure I did.

Nick had assured me that I'd love the convenience of the stackables right here in the house. And I hadn't argued because I'd spent years schlepping my laundry to the laundromat or to Gram's musty, cold, spidery basement.

When I was a kid, she had a wringer washer down there. Fascinating to watch her feed the wet clothes from the washing machine—an open-topped tub on wheels—through the rollers of the wringer. She warned me of the dangers of putting your fingers too close to the rollers. She told me how her friend, Mrs. O'Malley, once got her arm stuck in those rollers. I'd pictured Mrs. O'Malley with one regular arm and the other squeezed flat and much, much longer.

Nick was right about the convenience. It was important to be able to do my laundry at home since I had nobody to help tote things to and from the laundromat. Nobody to help an old spinster like me. Old Maid. Her face on the childhood deck of cards. Poor old lady. The aunt to everyone else's kids. Table for one at the restaurant. The One who will never be part of Two.

The comments were sure to come. "Poor Mackenzie. We all thought she'd be married and have a dozen children. We thought she'd be living happily ever after, but here she is, stuck in the carriage house, helping her grandmother take care of her third husband." (*Count 'em! Three husbands!*)

I let out a sigh just as Chloe sauntered into the bathroom and wrapped herself around my calves. I sat on the floor with my back against the washer and took her on my lap. She purred as I talked. "Gram's had three husbands, Chloe. I had one—Billy—but we got divorced. And then he died. Did I ever tell you that?"

She purred louder.

"Now here I am, living in this carriage house, doing my

laundry—nobody's underwear but my own—and taking care of you. This is my lot in life."

She looked up, and our eyes met. I said, "Oh, it's not that I don't love having you around." She laid her head in my lap and closed her eyes while I stroked her back. "You're a great friend," I said, but I was thinking about what she represented—the first of many, many cats I would have as I became Poor Mackenzie, Crazy Cat Lady.

And since I quit drinking, all I had left to soothe me, besides my cat, was sugar. I'd probably gain a ton of weight, which would make me even tastier for my dozen cats, who would eat me after I died alone in the carriage house.

I wanted a drink. Any drink as long as it was alcohol and guaranteed to numb what I was feeling. But all I had was half a bottle of Wollersheim wine under the kitchen sink, which I'd intended to pour out since I decided to take Nick's advice to give sobriety a try. Cold turkey.

Perfect Nick is all about abstinence, isn't he, Snarky said. *Abstinence. From everything.*

I'd asked—um, okay, I admit it—I *propositioned* Nick a few weeks back. He'd declined, saying he wanted us to be more committed before we did the deed. Rational Me could understand that, but Snarky thought it was a stupid idea. Lonely Me agreed.

Rational Me said, *If you want to be sober, pour the wine down the drain.*

Anxious countered with, *But we might really, really, really want some later.*

While they argued, I got up and put in the next load of laundry. And then, because I had nowhere to go and nobody to go there with anyway, I hit EXTRA RINSE. I was in no hurry.

I put on my yellow rubber gloves and started scrubbing the toilet. Poor Me.

Poor Toilet-Scrubbing-on-a-Saturday-Night Me.

CHAPTER ELEVEN

I HEARD A RAP ON the carriage house door and then Gram's voice as the door opened. "Yoo hoo! Anybody home?"

I came out of the bathroom, yellow gloves on. "Come in, Gram. I was just cleaning." I tossed the gloves under the kitchen sink, then washed my hands.

Gram was in her purple velour tracksuit, a vintage find she'd picked up at Lou's. Today she'd braided her longish gray hair and wound it into a tight roll at the top of her head. She set a plate decorated with little yellow chicks on my kitchen table. "I brought you some date nut bread and cream cheese." She held up a thermos. "And coffee."

Gram's date nut bread is to die for. It's dark, moist, and chewy with exactly enough chopped walnuts. It's particularly good slathered with cream cheese.

I poured two cups of coffee, and we sat at the kitchen table. Gram looked at me, and her little blue eyes filled with concern. "I saw you shaking your rugs outside earlier. You always clean when you're upset. What's going on, sweetie? Tell me, *kultaseni.*"

She called all of us kids kultaseni when I was growing up. She said the Finnish word meant that we were her "precious, darling sweethearts." Gram calls me sweetie or sometimes honey, but when she calls me kultaseni, it destroys me.

My lower lip quivered. I can be tough and badass and all detective-y, pretending to be okay when I'm not. I can do that with anyone else in the world, but not with Gram. I suddenly felt ten years old again. The tears flowed.

She rubbed my back while I sobbed and sniffled like a total wuss. After a few moments, she asked, gently, "Is it boy trouble?"

I nodded and gulped a breath. "Boys. Plural. I had two. Now I've got none." More tears. More back rubbing until I was finally able to pull it together.

I filled her in on Krissy hooking up with Vince. And Nick, out there with Bo Peep. I had to take a side trip in the conversation to explain why I called her Bo Peep, but we got back on track eventually.

Gram said, "You deserve better, sweetie."

I said, "Now you sound like my mother."

"Well, it's true. You deserve a loving relationship. These boys sound fickle to me. You deserve someone steady and faithful and true. Somebody who appreciates how wonderful you are."

"Yeah, sure," I said, "but where are they? Where are those men?" My friends and I had had many conversations about the men in our lives and how so many of them acted like overgrown adolescents, little boys in big boy bodies, preferring the company of video games and worse.

That wasn't true of Nick Milcross or Vince Hampton, of course, but they were rare in our age group. And now they were gone. I'd missed my chance.

I shoved a big chunk of date nut bread and cream cheese into my mouth.

Gram said, "Things have a way of working out. Did I ever tell you how your grandfather and I ended up together?"

My mouth full of cream cheese, I mumbled, "Remind me."

She sat back in her chair. "Well, he was dating someone else. A girl named Ethel. I don't know what he saw in her." Gram giggled, and her blue eyes twinkled with mischief as she leaned closer. "She had a long face. She looked a little bit like a horse."

I couldn't help but chuckle. And tried not to choke.

"Anyway, he and Horseface had been together for, oh, I guess a few months. And it was the night of the barn dance at the Lindelof farm. I was there with a very nice boy named—" She stopped and frowned. "Now isn't that something? I can't remember his name. He was tall and had lots of freckles." She knit her brows, concentrating on the plate of date nut bread. "What was his—?" She looked up, snapped her fingers. "Walter! His name was Walter Payne! Nice boy, but he didn't really, oh, you know what I mean. He didn't get my motor running."

I chuckled again, imagining Gram as a young girl with a running motor.

She went on. "So at the dance, the band played a polka. Then they said, 'Change partners!' You had to find someone else to dance with. And after a minute, they'd say it again."

"Sounds like fun," I said as I spread a huge gob of cream cheese on another piece of bread.

"Anyway, after a couple of changes, your grandfather and I ended up dancing. The polka ended, and they started a waltz. I expected he'd go back to Ethel, but he kept dancing with me." She sighed and smiled. "It was the Blue Danube Waltz. And he was humming along to it, and he had such a wonderful, deep voice. And those eyes of his. I'd never seen eyes quite that color, a gray blue, they were." She smiled bigger, looking toward the kitchen window.

I felt a warm glow listening to my grandmother reminisce. Such joy in her voice. I pictured Papa Powell, the way I remembered him. Tall, strong, and funny. He was so kind to us kids. I don't think I ever noticed his eyes, but I was only ten when he died.

Gram said, "I felt like I wanted to stay right there in his arms forever. And I think he must have been thinking the same thing. When the waltz ended, he looked at me." She grabbed my hand, looking directly into my eyes. "You know what it's like when someone *looks* at you? I mean *really* looks at you, like they can see something in you, something special. Something they like. It's a kind of electricity, that connection. Like a current running between you."

I sighed. "Like a spark." Like I saw with Krissy and Vince. *Stupid spark.* I shook off that image.

"Yes, yes." She nodded and picked up her coffee cup. "Yes, that's how he looked at me, and there was that spark."

"So how did you end up together? What happened to Horseface?"

She smiled. "Your grandpa called me the very next day. Told me he and Ethel were no longer seeing each other, and he asked me out. Just like that."

I smiled. "And the rest is history."

She nodded and smiled again. "Indeed."

We sat for a moment, eating date nut bread and drinking our coffees. Gram and Papa had been married for decades, had six children, and lived happily until he died tragically just before he planned to retire.

Gram said, "My point is you never know what's going

to happen. I went to that dance with Walter—a nice enough boy—and ended up with the man of my dreams. I often think what if I hadn't gone to the dance. What if I'd stayed home?"

"I'm glad you went. Otherwise, I wouldn't be here."

"Oh, you'd be here, but you'd be somebody else."

"So if I was somebody else, it means I wouldn't be here."

She frowned at me. "You know what I mean." Then she patted my hand. "Be patient, kultaseni. Be patient. God has a plan for you, and it will all work out in his good time. You'll see."

"So far, that plan hasn't worked out very well," I said, feeling perverse. I pulled my hand away.

Gram gave me a soft smile. "Life is long, Mackenzie. You're not even halfway through. Plenty of time for everything God has ordained to happen. Be patient." She took my hand and patted it again. "All in good time, kultaseni. All in good time."

Gram seemed confident in that "let go and let God" stuff, but to me it felt like no control, no choice. Like God would do what God would do, and I should just roll with that. It rankled me. I wanted to take charge and make things happen. But then again, doing things my way hadn't worked out so well.

Gram stood to leave. "Everything will work out. You'll see," she said.

Lonely Me doubted that. For now, my grandmother would have to have enough faith for both of us.

After Gram left, I took my stash of leftover Halloween candy to the couch and watched TV while I ate mini Snickers and bite-sized Almond Joys. Just the right combo of chocolate, caramel, and coconut to soothe my aching heart. And nuts for protein. Nuts are healthy, right?

I binged on the candy while I binge-watched Netflix—several episodes of a show where a woman about my age moves to New York. She lies about her age, pretending to be younger, gets a great job, and hooks up with a younger man. I watched this woman pretending to be somebody she was not, and I thought about Krissy, pretending to be my friend and then stealing my boyfriend.

Rational Me weighed in. *Vince is not your boyfriend.*

Lonely Me argued, *Well, no, but he could have been.*

Rational: *You don't know what really happened between them.*

Snarky gave a snort. *Yeah, right. We* saw *that spark.*

Lonely sighed. *Vince is gone. We'll just have to accept that.*

I turned off the TV and headed to bed before they could start talking about Nick. That would just have been too sad.

CHAPTER TWELVE

Sunday, November 23

ON SUNDAY AFTERNOONS, GRAM sets out a feast for anyone who comes to her table. This Sunday, it was Gram, Nathan, my mom, Duncan, and me. Gram invited Krissy, my aunt Fiona, and Fiona's friend, Harold, to join us.

We say "friend," but what is Harold exactly? Not her husband. Too old to be called a boyfriend.

Harold just sort of appeared one day a year or so ago. We're not quite sure where Fiona met him. My mother first saw Harold when she stopped by to talk to Fiona about something. As my mom described the scene later, there was Harold, sitting in a recliner in Fiona's living room, wearing one of those sleeveless white undershirts and boxer shorts, drinking beer and rolling his own cigarettes. My mom told us, "He barely said hello to me. He just sat there in his underwear, smoking and watching TV. He didn't even bother to go put on pants."

Despite that first impression, we all accept Harold. It's what our family does. Got a new boyfriend? He's welcome. You're divorced now? Your ex is still welcome, if you want them to be welcome. We don't judge. You love somebody new? We'll support you and probably come to love them too. Unless they break your heart. Then we'll reconsider. But only if you want us to.

I was in Gram's kitchen when Fiona, Harold, and Krissy got there. Harold shuffled past me, not even saying hello. He went straight to Gram's family room and sat on the couch. Fiona gave me a hug and then went into the dining room to talk to Gram.

When they were out of earshot, Kris said, "Harold didn't want to come, but my mom said he had to since I was in town. They had a huge fight about it driving over here in the camper. I think he hates the rest of the family, like he secretly resents that everyone is doing well."

Krissy was right. Of Gram's six children, only Fiona has had troubles in life. My mother says that's because Fiona is the baby of the family, and with five older siblings, she never learned to take care of herself.

I couldn't imagine what that was like. Middle kids like me are often lost in the shuffle of the family, and we learn early to take care of ourselves. We're not the perfect oldest child. (Hello, big sister Stephanie.) And we're not the darling youngest. (Yes, I mean you, baby sister Deanne.). I was stuck in the middle between older brother Greg, the jock, and younger brother Robbie, the joker.

I've had to make my own mark on the world, and I'm trying to do that now as an officially licensed investigator with Tri-Mak. Which, when I think about it, might make me the coolest of the siblings. Not that I'm keeping track.

And if Harold doesn't like us, tough. His loss.

Before Kris and I went into the dining room, I had to ask.

I tried to keep my voice neutral, even though I wanted to yell. "So, Krissy? You and Vince?"

She looked at me, and I knew instantly that they'd spent the night together. You can just tell when someone's had a really good time.

She gave me a shy smile as she nodded. "Yeah. Vince. Wow."

Back in middle school, Vince used to tease me. He still does. I've always pretended to hate it, but his teasing me was one of "our" things. Vince's and mine. And now someone else was enjoying, uh, *new* things with him. And though Vince and I had only kissed a few times, I had imagined doing more than just kissing more than once. A *lot* more than once.

And now Krissy had experienced what I'd only imagined.

My cheeks felt hot. I resisted the urge to ask how it was. How he was. Or punch her in the face. I resisted all that.

She frowned. "You look upset. It's okay, isn't it, that he and I, you know? He told me you were just friends. That you and he weren't—"

I waved a hand. "No problem. He's right. We're just friends." My stomach knotted when I said that. *Liar, liar, liar.*

She leaned back. "Okay, good. That's what he told me, and I just wanted to be sure. And I gotta say, I'm really glad it's true. Really, *really* glad." Her cheeks reddened.

I didn't know what to say. I sure didn't need any details of just how really, *really* glad Vince had made my cousin feel, so I just offered a lame, "I'm happy for you."

One of those times you say something like that, but you do not mean it. Not. At. All.

I changed the subject. "Did you find the bones, Krissy?"

Her face got pink, and she looked away. "I, uh, didn't have time to even look. We were, uh, busy until early this morning."

Busy. With Vince. Ugh!

Gram called us to the table. Snarky was relieved to not have to look at Krissy's stupid face or think about her and stupid Vince being stupid busy all night.

Gram had prepared one of her amazing Sunday dinners—roast beef with mashed potatoes, perfect gravy, glazed carrots, baking powder biscuits, and for dessert, a coconut custard pie with Gram's usual mile-high meringue.

I took a huge forkful of pie and let it melt away on my tongue. "Gram," I said, "if you went on one of those TV baking shows, you'd win with this pie, hands down."

Fiona said, "I love those shows, and Mackenzie is right, Ma. You'd win."

Gram beamed.

Harold, who had scarfed down his dinner without talking to any of us, declined to have pie. He stood, gave a stiff, brief "thank you and goodbye" to Gram, and left. Socially awkward, yes, or maybe he was just seriously introverted. Or maybe, as Kris suggested, he just hated us.

I followed him out the back door. "Harold, wait!"

He turned toward me on the driveway. "What?"

I said, "Krissy said you tried to fix her car, is that right?"

He nodded. "I found some sparkplugs in the trunk and replaced them. But it didn't help much."

Huzzah! Harold had opened Krissy's trunk. "Did you find a burlap bag in the trunk?"

He leveled a look at me and waited a beat before answering. "Maybe."

I put on my most serious detective face. "Did you find a bag or not?"

He muttered something.

I got louder. "Harold! If you found a burlap bag in that trunk, you have to tell me what you did with it. If you don't, the police will arrest you."

He scowled. "For what?"

I got in his face and hissed. "Concealing a corpse. Five years in prison. Minimum." I had no idea if that was true, but the words had the desired effect on Harold.

He held up both hands in surrender. "I didn't know what Kris had gotten herself into. So I stuck the bag in the garage until I could figure out what else to do. What am I supposed to do with it now?"

"Absolutely nothing! Leave the bag right where it is. This is a federal case now," I lied. Again. I was getting very, very good at lying. "Do you understand?"

I watched the color drain from his face. He looked like he was going to pass out. Voice soft, he asked, "Whose bones are they?"

I shrugged. "I don't know, but whatever you do, don't touch them."

He gave his head a hard shake. "Not a chance. Stuff like that gives me the heebie-jeebies."

I told him to take the camper and go home. "I'll bring Fiona and Kris back to the house later. And remember? Don't touch the bones. Got it?"

He nodded and left.

I rejoined the family at the table. Nobody seemed upset that Harold was gone. All Gram said was, "Oh, dear, that's too bad he didn't get any dessert." And Fiona said, "Oh well, more pie for me," as she helped herself to a second piece.

I took another piece too.

Nathan had gone upstairs for a nap. My mother was talking

about wedding plans to Duncan, who sat beside her, picking away at the last of the pie on his plate, smiling and nodding as she talked.

My mom said, “I’ve always wanted a spring wedding. Or Valentine’s Day? What do you think, Dunc?” Before he could answer, she chattered on. “Or how about New Year’s Eve, and we can start the year married?” She looked at me. “The time of year that you have the wedding affects everything. The whole theme, the colors, the flowers. Everything. If it’s around Valentine’s Day, we can go the pink, red, and white route. If it’s in the spring, then it’s all about the pastels. If we wait until next fall, then it’s autumn colors. Yellow. Orange.”

I mmm-hummed as I ate my pie, trying not to picture how hideous I’d look in some poofy orange bridesmaid dress.

She went on. “If we get married next winter, then frosty silver and blue. Those are lovely colors, but the flower choices aren’t as unlimited as other times of the year.” She looked blissful, her eyes sparkling and cheeks flushed. She gave a big sigh and looked back at Duncan. “It’s all so complicated, isn’t it, hon?”

Duncan shrugged. “As long as I’m your husband at the end of it, I’ll be happy.” He put his hand behind her head and pulled her into a kiss.

Romantic Me smiled. *Aw, that Duncan. He always says the right thing.*

Lonely Me sighed. *Wish we had a Duncan.*

CHAPTER THIRTEEN

I'D FINISHED MY PIE and sat mooning over my mother's relationship with Duncan, the Vince-Krissy thing, and my sad lack of anything like that in my life, when Krissy leaned over to me and said, "My mom is ready to go, if you are. Head to your place?"

I felt another little twinge that might have been jealousy before Badass Me snapped. *For God's sake! Enough feeling sorry for yourself. Let it go. Get back to work!*

Oh yeah. Work. Fiona. Money. Bones.

My grandmother had gone upstairs to join Nathan. My mother said she and Duncan would take cleanup duty. Krissy and Fiona followed me across Gram's driveway and the backyard to the carriage house. As I opened the door, I said, "Welcome to my office."

Fiona looked around and said, "Cute place. And so clean."

Consider the source, Snarky snarked. She can be so mean sometimes.

"Thanks," I said. My place always looks great after I've angry-cleaned. I didn't want Krissy to know she was the reason for that. I brought a yellow legal pad and pen to the table, and the three of us sat.

Fiona's hands shook as she asked, "Got anything to drink? You know Ma doesn't allow it." She was right. Gram doesn't drink alcohol—never has.

I got Fiona a wine glass and took the Wollersheim Prairie Sunburst out from under the sink. I poured some into Fiona's glass, stopping halfway, giving her a questioning look.

"Keep going," she said. She glugged that down and said, "Hit me again." I drained the bottle and put it in my recycle bag under the sink. Fiona drained the glass and set it back on the table with a satisfying thump. "That's better," she said and leaned back in her chair.

Fiona spent the next ten minutes telling me about her life as the baby of the family. "I was a cutie pie, with my curly blonde hair and dimples. 'Little Shirley,' they called me. Like Shirley Temple, you know? Everybody's darling."

I remembered watching the old movies with Gram, with Shirley Temple singing "On the Good Ship Lollipop."

Fiona said, "But then you get older, like those child stars, and you're not so cute anymore. People start treating you differently."

I said, "Aunt Fiona, I've seen pictures of you in Gram's photo albums. You as a kid, in high school, and from your wedding. You always were, and still are, beautiful." I patted her arm.

Krissy rolled her eyes and looked at the ceiling.

Fiona shook her head. "No. No, I am not. I've gotten old, and I'm a mess." She ran her hands over her cheeks, pulling the skin back, away from her mouth. She looked at me. "See? This is who I used to be." She let go, and the skin sagged back into wrinkles. "This is who I am now."

Years of hard drinking had left her face sallow and heavily lined. Her youthful spark was definitely gone. She seemed sad, depressed, and hopeless.

She said, "I never went to college, you know. I went to work waiting tables at Donatello's right after high school."

I smiled. "I remember you working there. You were great at that. So fast and efficient."

She shrugged off the compliment. "Well, that kind of work takes its toll. And there was a lot of partying among the staff after hours. Hard work. Late nights. Eventually I just wore out. My feet couldn't take it anymore. I gave it up four years ago, but I miss the hustle and bustle of the restaurant. I miss seeing new people."

"So what do you do now?"

"Oh, a little of this and a little of that."

Krissy gave a snort and stood up, pressing both hands on the table as she leaned toward her mother. "Oh, for the love of God, Ma, quit sugar coating it! You spend your days drinking and shopping online and on that frickin' shopping channel on TV. You can hardly walk through your house—you have so much crap in there!"

Fiona stood up fast and slammed a palm against the table. It was almost comical to see five-foot-two Fiona going head-to-head with her five-foot-ten daughter.

She glared up, poking her index finger at Krissy to emphasize each syllable. "You. Shut. Your. Damn. Mouth! Don't you dare speak to me that way!"

Krissy tensed. I tensed, expecting a battle. Then Kris relaxed, sighed, and sat down at the table. She muttered, "Sorry, Mother."

I had a glimpse of the power little Fiona must have wielded over her daughter and likely her late husband as well.

Fiona sat back in her chair and pointed to her empty wine glass. "You have any more of that?"

"Sorry, no. That was it." I brought her a glass of water. She took a long drink, and when I sensed she was calmer, I asked, "How can you afford to shop like you do?"

She gave me a hard look, and I was afraid she was going to yell at me like she'd yelled at Krissy. But she took a breath and said, "I saved. I saved. I saved. All my tips. Every extra penny. Your uncle Andy made a good living, and he handled all the finances. And he had a good insurance policy when he died. I have few expenses, just my food."

I heard Krissy mutter, "And your booze," but Fiona either didn't hear that or chose to ignore her daughter. Either way, I was grateful to avoid another flare of temper.

"Krissy mentioned that you've gotten yourself into some debt. That someone is harassing you. Any ideas who it might be?"

Fiona gave an exasperated sigh. She dripped sarcasm. "Well, if I knew who it was, I wouldn't need your help, would I?"

Krissy said, "Stop, Ma! Mackenzie is just trying to help you. Don't get snotty with her."

Fiona's cheeks colored. "I didn't mean anything."

I shrugged it off. "No sweat. So do you have any ideas why you're being harassed?"

Fiona got quiet as she twirled the stem of her wine glass, swirling the dregs. "Well, I've gotten myself into a financial hole somehow. Spent what I had."

Kris gave a grunt of disgust.

Fiona glared at her. "I've had to *live*, you know!" She turned back to me. "I honestly don't know what happened, Mackenzie. I owe people money now. And this guy named Wally Klemish might be a little upset with me. He has one of those payday loan places where you promise them your paycheck if they lend you some money." She looked down at the table and said, quietly, "I don't have a paycheck, so I put up my car. I haven't been able to pay him back."

I grabbed my cell, Googled, and found an address for E-Z MONEY on the south side of Three Rivers, not far from Target. "Okay, I'll have a talk with Mr. Klemish. Is there anyone else who might be, uh, unhappy with you?"

She fiddled with her glass again, eyes downcast. "Mrs. McGruder isn't too thrilled with me these days. I've complained about her chickens. Filthy beasts!"

Krissy piped up. "That old bat next door? She was a total witch back when I was a kid. I'm surprised you haven't killed each other by now."

I made notes. "Who is this person, and why the hard feelings?"

Fiona said, "She accused me of flirting with her husband years ago—as if I had any interest in that tub of lard she was married to! Ridiculous!" She looked at Krissy. "Your father was my one true love. I never looked at another man as long as we were married."

Krissy patted Fiona's arm. "I know, Ma. You guys loved each other. That was obvious."

I wondered about that since we'd all heard about the battles Aunt Fiona and Uncle Andy had. Steering the conversation to current events, I asked, "Why would this Mrs. McGruder be mad at you now? Both of your husbands are long gone."

"I know she talks about me to the other neighbors. Says that I'm a tramp. A hoarder. A drunk. She just has it in for me, and she's never going to change."

"Has she made any direct threats, or is it just gossiping behind your back?"

"She called the city on me more than once, complaining about the weeds in my yard. For the love of God, my lawnmower was broken. I tried to get somebody to come and take care of it. It wasn't until I met Harold that the lawn got mowed. That's how we met. He stopped by the house one day and asked if I wanted some help with the lawn. He said he'd be glad to do the grass. He did such a nice job, and I invited him in for a beer when he was done."

Krissy said, "Tell her the whole story, Ma."

Fiona scowled at Kris, then looked at me. "Harold needed some money to start his business, so I lent him what he needed."

Krissy said, "Tell her how much you gave him, Ma."

Fiona cleared her throat, looked at the ceiling, then looked at Krissy, fire in her eyes. "It's none of anyone's business how much I gave him. And it has nothing to do with anything, so let's just drop it!"

Krissy turned to me. "She doesn't want to tell you that she gave Harold almost ten grand to start this business of his." She looked at her mother. "And what exactly is his business, Ma?"

Fiona pressed her lips together.

Krissy hit her fist against the table. "Tell her, or I will."

Fiona glared at Krissy, then looked at me. "It's all perfectly legal, perfectly legitimate."

Krissy scoffed and looked away.

Fiona said, "He arranges things for people."

I asked, "What kind of things?"

She paused, then said, "Marriages."

I sat back in my chair. This was a new one. "What? How does he do this exactly?"

Fiona said, “He has a website. Men in this country, seeking wives from other countries. Women overseas who want to start a new life in the United States.”

I said nothing for a moment, wondering how anyone would need ten grand to set up a website.

Fiona broke the silence. “He arranges for men and women to meet. He’s the middleman. Like a dating service, except the expectation is that you get married.”

“And people pay for this?”

“Oh yes. The men pay him for the service. The women don’t pay anything.”

“And he’s successful at this?”

“Well, yes. More or less.”

This opened another line of possibility. Maybe Fiona wasn’t the target of the harassment. Maybe it was Harold. “Anyone angry with him over failed relationships?”

“There was one man who complained, but I’m not sure about anyone else.”

“Do you know who the man is, how I can reach him?”

“You’d have to ask Harold.”

I made a note to do just that.

CHAPTER FOURTEEN

FIONA NEEDED TO USE the bathroom. Krissy said she needed a cigarette. I sat alone at the table, thinking. On the list of "who's mad at Fiona," I had Wally Klemish, to whom she owed money, and her neighbor Mrs. McGruder, who'd been an enemy for years. And maybe a disgruntled "customer" of Harold's. Maybe the harassment was actually aimed at Harold and not at Fiona at all.

I felt a little buzzing in my head, the feeling I always have when I'm trying to figure out who did what to whom and why. Especially the why. What drives people to do what they do?

I observed a lot growing up. I watched my older siblings navigate life, learning and following the rules. I watched my younger siblings break the rules and get by with it. Brother Robbie could always talk his way out of trouble. Little Deanne just needed to look like she was about to cry, and she'd avoid punishment.

In the middle, I learned the rules and also learned to bend them as needed. Especially in the name of fairness. And now in my investigator role, I'm about justice. I want to find answers, bring people closure, see evil punished.

In the process, I've been in danger myself many times. All in the service of truth.

What was the truth here? Truth: Someone was harassing my aunt, and I intended to find out who and why. Truth: Someone had stolen from my cousin. Who? Why? Truth: Someone had left a bag of bones in the trunk of a car. Who? Why? And those bones *were* someone, and that person—whoever he or she was—deserved to be identified and laid to rest. And their family deserved to know what happened to them.

Krissy came in from outside, smelling of smoke. She went to the counter and took the last piece of Gram's date nut bread.

Fiona came out of the bathroom, dug through her big handbag, and brought out a sheaf of papers. "Maybe this will help," she said. "It's the paperwork from the loan place."

The first paper was an official-looking contract from E-Z MONEY. "Your signature is clear, but whoever signed from the business is illegible."

The next thing in the stack was an insurance policy. I asked, "You bought kidnap and ransom insurance?"

Fiona said, "Well, you never know when you might be kidnapped. The nice man on the phone said so. He wanted me to get cremation insurance too. You know, in case I was ever accidentally cremated."

I bit back a laugh, but Krissy could not. She snort-laughed and then held her sides as she walked around the room, trying to get it under control. Finally, she made it back to the table. She said, "Ma! Think about it. How do you get accidentally cremated?" She burst out laughing again.

Fiona got very quiet, then said, "You think you're so smart."

I said, "She's just teasing you, Aunt Fiona. But there are people taking advantage of older people out there, manipulating them into buying things. Scamming them for bank account numbers, stealing identities. You have to be really careful these days."

She rolled her eyes. "I know that!" Her cheeks reddened. "He talked really fast, and before I knew it . . ." She looked down at the table.

Krissy patted her on the back. "It's okay, Ma. You didn't know."

Everyone calm, I said, "Tell me what's been going on so we can help you figure all this out."

Fiona took a deep breath, let it out, and opened with, "I don't want your grandmother to know about any of this. Promise you'll keep it between us?" She reached into her bag, pulled out a dollar, and laid it on the table. "There. I'm officially hiring you. There's some kind of investigator-client confidentiality, right? So your grandma won't hear any of this, right?"

I didn't want to tell her that the relationship between investigator and client didn't carry the same guarantees of confidentiality as, say, attorney-client privilege, but there are ethical guidelines that require us to protect information.

I said, "I promise. Gram would just worry." I resisted adding that my grandmother would probably want to "help" investigate—or worse, rope her friend Velma into helping her help me—and then things could get very messy indeed. Things could go south fast. Very fast.

Fiona clasped her hands tightly on the table in front of her. "Okay then. It started with phone calls."

"On your landline?" In our little town, lots of people still have landlines, especially people of a certain age.

"Yes. I don't have a cell phone anymore. They were hangups or sometimes breathing and then hanging up."

"You don't have caller ID?"

"No. I never bothered with that. I just stopped answering the phone. They never left a message. Then other things started happening. One morning, a pile of dog crap on the front steps. A big pile. Obviously from a very large dog."

I made a note of that on my notepad: *Who has large dog?*

"The next day, there was a dead bird on the back steps."

"What kind of bird?"

"A robin. I felt bad about that. Robins never hurt anything. If it had been a dead crow, I wouldn't have been one bit sorry. Crows are the worst, aren't they? So noisy and always harassing other birds. Just the other day—"

I held up a hand to stop what was sure to be a long story from Fiona. "You don't have any security cameras?" I knew it was a ridiculous question the second I uttered it. A person with a landline and no caller ID isn't likely to have a security system.

Fiona scoffed. "Of course not. Why would I need that?"

Krissy gave a huff. "Duh! Think about it, Ma!" She stopped when I shot her a cautioning look and a small shake of my head that telegraphed, "Not helping."

Krissy gave another huff of disgust and went into the bathroom.

Fiona's voice got shaky. "Who is doing this to me?"

I shrugged. "I don't know, Aunt Fiona, but I'll try to find out. Has there been anything else?"

She swallowed hard, blinking back tears. "The worst one was just a couple days ago. I got up in the morning, and there was a noose in the plum tree."

"What kind of noose?"

"The kind you see in the old Westerns. A rope about this thick." She made a circle with her thumb and index finger. "Hanging right there in my plum tree. I took it down before the neighbors could see it."

Fiona had imagined things before. "What did you do with the rope?"

"I threw it in the garbage can behind the garage."

"Has your trash been picked up since then?" If I had the rope, I might be able to trace it back to a purchaser. At least that's how it works on TV.

"Yes, later that same day the truck came."

That meant the noose was in the Ten Mile Landfill, and I'd spent enough time there in the past. I wasn't going to go digging for a noose.

Fiona gave a sigh. "I should have kept it. You could check for fingerprints."

I shook my head. "Not likely there'd be usable prints on that rough surface." Snarky whispered, *Impressive. You sound like a real detective.*

Fiona looked forlorn. "Even so, I should have kept it, huh?"

Krissy had come back to the table in time to hear that. "Yeah, Ma! You should have kept it. Duh!"

Fiona glared at her. "No need to be snotty, Kris. I'm doing my best here!"

I raised my voice to short-circuit the argument. "And even if we could get a print, there'd be no guarantee that it belonged to whoever hung the rope. No idea how many people handled it before someone made the noose."

Fiona shot Krissy a self-satisfied look.

Krissy rolled her eyes and went to the refrigerator. "Got any beer?"

"Sorry, no. Just Diet Coke."

She took a can, opened it, took a big slug, let out a belch, and went to the couch. Chloe jumped up next to her. The two of them settled into Chloe's favorite routine: you pet, I purr.

I made notes to talk to Fiona's neighbors to see if anyone saw anything suspicious or if anyone else had noticed dead animals. In the process, I might be able to tell if one of them was harassing her. "Are there any feral cats in the neighborhood who might have killed the robin and brought it to you as a gift?" I gestured toward the couch. "Chloe used to do that all the time. Birds, half-eaten baby rabbits, field mice. Left them for me, like she was leaving me the best presents imaginable."

Fiona said, "Any cats that might be around, Mr. Rooney's dogs would chase them away. I'm sure of that." She explained that Mr. Rooney and his two Rottweilers lived next door to the east. I made a note to talk with him.

"Have you heard the dogs barking during the night recently—especially on the nights when things happened?" Those dogs would likely raise a ruckus if anyone were skulking around during the night.

She shook her head. "Haven't heard a peep from them. Not even their usual nighttime barking. Every night at bedtime, he lets them out, and they give a few barks. Makes me smile thinking they are just letting us all know it's time for bed."

The dogs wouldn't bark at their owner, so that put Mr. Rooney on the suspect list. Rottweilers are big, and so are their, uh, deposits. "Could Mr. Rooney be responsible for harassing you?"

She shook her head. "Why would he? We've always gotten along very well. In fact, I'm pretty sure he's sweet on me."

Krissy gave a snort. "Sweet on you, Ma? You've always thought any man who was breathing was after you."

Fiona glared at her. "He sent me flowers after your father died. You probably don't remember that!"

Kris scoffed. "Ugh! With a *sympathy* card, Ma! He felt *sorry* for you!"

Fiona huffed back at Krissy. "Trust me. I know when a man is interested!"

Krissy jumped up. Chloe dove off the couch with a meow of protest and headed upstairs to my bedroom.

Kris came to the table and stood over her mother. "Ma! You are ridiculous! You've always been like this. Mack is trying to help you, and you're all caught up in your fantasy world where everybody loves you!" She bent down until they were nose to nose. "Listen to me. Everybody does *not* love you. Someone *hates* you. Hates you *a lot.* Enough to threaten you. They hung that noose in the tree as a warning. A noose, Mother, a *noose*! You *get* it? They want you *dead*!"

Fiona started to shake. "I know, I know. I'm terrified, if you want to know the truth. Terrified!" She threw her arms around her daughter's waist and sobbed. Big, shuddering sobs.

After a moment, Krissy hugged her, rubbing her back. Her voice soft and soothing, Kris said, "It's okay, Ma. We'll figure this out. Mackenzie and I will figure it out. It's going to be okay."

I wondered how often Krissy had taken this role of supportive parent to her immature mother during her childhood.

Another few moments of nurturing and comforting, and Fiona let go, sat back, and grabbed a napkin from the holder on the table. She wiped her eyes and blew her nose, then shoved the napkin inside her left sleeve. She gave a weak chuckle. "Sorry about that, girls."

I smiled at her. "Totally understandable. Anyone would be overwhelmed in your situation."

She met my eyes. "Thanks for trying to help, Mackenzie. I appreciate it."

Krissy, standing behind her mother, gave me a big shrug and one of those looks that said, clearly, "What about me? Don't I get any thanks?"

As if she sensed Krissy's silent communication, Fiona turned and grabbed Krissy's hand. "Oh, and you too, Kristen. Thanks for coming home to help me."

Krissy patted her on the shoulder. "It's okay, Ma. It's all going to be okay."

I hoped Kris was right.

CHAPTER FIFTEEN

I DROVE KRIS AND HER mother back to Fiona's house around four that afternoon. We pulled into the driveway and, as Fiona got out of the back seat, she glanced into the back of Cricket. She gave a shriek and yelled, "Kristen, is that what I think it is? Is that my *suitcase*?"

Krissy looked like she wanted to throw up. She whispered, "Oh crap," and got out of the car. I listened from the drivers' seat—not willing to enter the war zone—as they screamed at each other in the driveway. Fiona accused Kris of disrespecting her property. Kris tried to defend herself. Finally, Fiona swore and stomped into the house.

I got out of the car and went to Krissy's side. She lit a Camel and leaned against the back of the car, sucking in smoke and letting it out slowly. "I told you she'd be upset."

I nodded. "You were right about that." My poor cousin.

After Kris finished her cigarette, I told her that Harold had put the bones in the garage. We walked to the detached garage behind the house. The side door stood open, and a snuffling sound came from inside the garage.

In a flash, a Rottweiler raced past us, dragging a burlap bag. A second Rottweiler followed, hot on his heels as they tore down the alley. Likely Mr. Rooney's dogs, on the loose.

I yelled at Kris. "Catch that dog!"

She shot me a look that said I was delusional. We sprinted after them. As the dogs ran, a bone flew out of the bag. Kris ran on while I paused to pick up the femur. I caught up to her after pausing to pick up a clavicle. Or maybe it was a scapula.

We reached the neighbor's backyard at the end of the block. The burlap bag was snagged at the bottom of a lilac bush.

One of the dogs had the end of the bag in his teeth, growling. Krissy pulled the other end free and held on, snarling back. A tug of war ensued.

I yelled, "Here boy! Fetch!" I waved the femur as if I were going to throw it. He let go of the burlap sack and stood at the ready, tail high, tongue hanging out, panting in anticipation. His pal did the same. Twins.

I quickly stooped down and picked up a fat stick lying by the bushes. "Fake out!" I yelled as I threw the stick instead of the bone. Both dogs took off after it. One got it, and they argued for a moment before the loser gave in and followed the victor back toward Fiona's.

I ran to where Krissy was sitting on the grass, clutching the burlap sack to her chest, breathing heavily. I sat next to her, catching my breath.

Krissy said, "That's the most exercise I've had in months. Didn't realize how out of shape I've gotten."

Rational Me so wanted to say, *Smoking doesn't help*, but I resisted. I know how thrilled I am when people talk about my bad habits. *Yes, Mother, I eat too many sweets. Yes, Nick, occasionally I drink too much. Yeah, yeah, yeah, people. Leave me alone.*

I stood and pulled Krissy to her feet. "That was quite the workout. That dog was really committed to that bag of bones. We'd better backtrack and make sure no other bones fell out while we were chasing him."

Krissy carried the burlap sack up the alley. I picked up an ulna next to a garbage can. Or it might have been a radius. Or maybe a fibula. Hard to tell.

Kris said, "Super treat for a dog—not just one bone, but a bag full of them."

"Yeah," I said. "Like Christmas morning for a mutt." We reached Fiona's house. "Let's put these somewhere safer. Not in the garage, obviously."

Krissy asked, "Can't we just dump the bones in the landfill? Or there's a national forest north of here. We could bury the bag there."

"What if some animal decides to dig it up and the bones are traced back to us?" I honestly didn't know how that could happen, but I was absolutely sure that someday, somehow, Krissy would get in trouble for it. And then so would I.

My mother was right. Krissy finds trouble, or trouble finds her. That's just Kris.

I suggested that we put the bones in Fiona's basement, where Krissy had put the burlap bag full of money. "The bones will be safe enough there until we can talk to the chief."

We went to Fiona's basement. Kris led the way past the washer and dryer, through a maze of boxes, old furniture, and other stuff crammed down there, to the back corner where the furnace stood. She stepped around the furnace. "The money is right back here—" She stopped. She swore.

I stepped next to her and looked down. No burlap bag.

"It's gone. My money is gone," she said. She looked at me, eyes wide, then her shock turned to fury. She ran up the steps to the kitchen screaming, "Mother! What have you done?"

I followed Kris up the steps and sat at the kitchen table, setting the bag of bones on the floor by my feet. I cringed as round two of the fight commenced in the living room.

The daughter, screaming and swearing at the mother. The mother, screaming and swearing at the daughter. All this happening with such ease, so well-practiced. This was another glimpse into life with Fiona, and it was not pretty. Especially for Kris, growing up here.

I waited in the kitchen until things settled down. At least the fight hadn't gotten physical. Kris stormed into the kitchen, unleashing a string of epithets about her mother. "She took the bag to the casino last night and lost it all. Lost it all! How could she do that to me?" She sucked in a deep breath and then ramped up again. "She claims she didn't know it was mine. Claims Harold told her it was his, that he'd been saving up to surprise her. What a crock! She's a liar and a thief! Why did I even come home? What was I thinking?"

She plopped onto one of the wooden kitchen chairs, gave a groan, crossed her arms on the table, and laid her head down on her arms. She moaned again.

I took a glass from the cupboard, filled it with tap water, and set it in front of her as I patted her shoulder. "Here. Drink some water. Take a breath."

She lifted her head, took a sip. She fought tears. "Mack, it's always been this way. Total disrespect for everyone else. Just doing what she feels like and damn the consequences."

I sat back down at the table just as Fiona stomped into the kitchen, carrying a burlap bag. She threw it at Krissy's feet. "Here! Take it and get out, you selfish brat!" She stomped back out of the room.

I opened the bag. Several bundles of cash were there. "Krissy, look. Your money is still here."

She emptied the bag onto the table. "It's not *all* here. Not even half!" She picked up a bundle of twenties and threw it back down. "Damn her!"

Krissy yelled into the other room, launching a barrage of F-bombs in her mother's direction. "What the ever-lovin' f—k, Ma! You lost almost all of *my* f—king money! You had no f—king right!"

Fiona shouted back. "Well, you stole my suitcase! And I didn't take all the money! I just took a little to the casino! I was keeping the rest for emergencies!"

Kris looked at me. "Emergencies? That's a laugh. Her next emergency would be another trip to the casino, or the next sparkly thing she sees on the shopping channel."

I said, "Or maybe more cremation insurance?" Trying to lighten the mood.

Krissy stared at me a second and then gave a snort. "The woman is nuts!"

I said, "So what do you want to do? You want her arrested for theft?" I was sure the chief could arrange for someone to put the fear of God into Fiona for taking her daughter's money. Even though that money was ill-gotten gain from an illegal casino. But I didn't need to go down that rabbit hole at the moment.

Krissy gave a grunt. "Arrest her? Hell no. Why bother? She's going to do whatever she wants to do. She's never going to change. But right now, I can't stand to even look at her. I just might strangle her." Her fists clenched at her sides. She had murder in her eyes.

"How about you stay at my place until we figure this out?" I didn't want Krissy to be arrested for matricide.

She agreed and grabbed her clothes from the living room, then cleared her things from the main floor bathroom, stuffing them all into a white trash bag. We brought that bag, the sack of bones, and the burlap bag of what was left of the money to Cricket.

I called Jimmy's and ordered a pizza to go. An hour later, we were in the carriage house, eating pizza and relaxing on the couch, Chloe curled between us. We watched an old sitcom on Hulu from our younger days—a group of girls having hilarious adventures in a private school.

It felt good to laugh. At the end of the fifth episode, Krissy stood, stretched, and yawned. "I'm wiped out," she said. "Fighting with Fiona is always exhausting."

I'd put both burlap bags under the bathroom sink for the night. "Tomorrow morning, we'll hide the bags in Gram's basement. That old Victorian house has a lot of basement hidey-holes. I'll tell Gram so she won't be surprised if she finds them down there."

Kris said, "And my mother won't go snooping there."

"Right, and tomorrow after breakfast, we'll go to TriMak and ask the chief for his advice."

My turn to stretch and yawn. It was after eleven, and I was exhausted. I brought Krissy a pillow and a couple blankets and said goodnight.

She smiled at me. "Thanks for all your help, cuz. You're the best. Sleep tight."

I added, "Don't let the bedbugs bite," just as a cockroach ran out from under the pile of clothes Kris had dumped on the floor. A refugee from Fiona's. "Get that bug!" I yelled.

Krissy jumped up. "I'll stomp it!"

Before she could, Chloe pounced and made quick work of the little bugger. Chloe looked quite delighted with herself, purring as Kris sang her praises.

I left the two of them curled together on the couch and went upstairs to bed, trying not to imagine what Chloe would do if she ever got hold of Jimbo.

CHAPTER SIXTEEN

Monday, November 24, 1:00 a.m.

KRISSY SHOOK ME AWAKE at one in the morning. "My mother called. She's hysterical." We got to Fiona's ten minutes later. The back screen door and the door into her kitchen were both wide open, despite the near-freezing temperature outside.

I called out as we entered. "Aunt Fiona? It's Mack. I'm here." Krissy closed the doors behind us.

Fiona came running from the other room and threw her arms around me. "Thank God you're here, Mackenzie. It was horrible. Just horrible!" She ignored Krissy.

Get the facts first. Speculate later.

Fiona's words came in a rush. "I heard a scuffling sound in the bedroom. I opened my eyes, and a huge crow was in my room!" She moved her arms, demonstrating how it swooped over her bed and then perched on top of the drapes. Her eyes got big. "It sat up there staring at me. Like the raven in that Poe thing. Just staring at me."

I slowed my speech, hoping she'd slow hers. "What did you do then?"

Her words continued to tumble out. "I ran out of the bedroom, down the stairs. It chased me!" Breathless now, she said, "I ran to the front door, and it flew out." She plopped down into a kitchen chair, her hands shaking. "It was terrifying!"

Krissy said, "Are you *sure* it was real, Ma? Sure it wasn't one of your spells?"

Fiona sat up straight and looked at her daughter, as if realizing for the first time Krissy was in the room. "Spells? Spells?" She smacked a palm on the table. "I wish to God this family would stop talking about me having spells! I can tell you that thing was real. Absolutely real!" She looked at me. "I called Kristen so you could get over here and figure out who is doing this to me!"

I said, "Your back door was open when I got here. Did you know that?"

Fiona looked confused. "It was open? No, I didn't leave it open. I'd never do that."

I asked, "Where *is* Harold?"

She gave a lip curl. "In the camper, I assume."

I sat at the table, took Fiona's hand. Looked her in the eye. "Aunt Fiona, were you and Harold fighting earlier?" Perhaps he'd decided to exact a little revenge, crow-style.

"Well, yes, but he wouldn't have let that nasty bird in here. He knows I'm terrified of crows."

If Harold was responsible for this latest incident, maybe he'd been responsible for the others as well. But what motive would he have?

Krissy said, "Speak of the devil."

A sleepy Harold came in through the back door. "Wuzz goin' on?" He rubbed at his eyes. He reeked of stale beer.

Fiona told him about the crow.

"What? A crow? How'd it get in?"

I said, "The back door was open."

"Aw, geez. That would be my fault. I propped the doors open when I carried some stuff out to the camper."

Fiona glared at him. "What stuff? Are you taking *my* stuff?"

He frowned at her. "Jesus, calm down. We've got company."

I intervened. "So you left the doors open, Harold?"

"Yeah, I forgot to come back and shut 'em." He looked at Fiona, then hung his head. "Sorry about that." She huffed, turned her back on him, and crossed her arms.

While she pouted, I focused—as much as I could on only a couple hours of sleep. Harold had explained the open doors, but what were the odds a crow would randomly fly into the house in the middle of the night? A bat, maybe, or even an owl, since those are nocturnal. But a crow? Not likely. I asked, "Did you notice anyone outside earlier, Harold?"

He shook his head. "Nah, I've been asleep. I got up a minute ago to get a drink of water and saw the kitchen lights on over here."

Krissy muttered, "Water? That's a laugh."

I ignored her and continued with Harold. "You didn't hear any noises? Or see someone walking on the driveway, maybe?"

"Nope. I sleep like I'm dead."

Krissy whispered, "More like passing out."

Fiona was getting hysterical. "I saw it! It was real, and it was huge. It attacked me in my sleep—swooping and cawing. Scared me to death!"

I decided the best approach was to actually investigate. *Duh. Brilliant, Sherlock.* Snarky can be nasty in the middle of the night. "Can you show me what happened?"

Fiona led me to the stairway as she repeated her story. "I ran down here. It came after me. I ran to the front door, opened it, and the crow flew out."

I crossed the entryway to the front door. "Maybe it left a feather somewhere." I saw nothing.

I followed Fiona up to her bedroom. No feathers on the steps either. The pale green walls of her bedroom were hidden behind the piles of boxes and bins that lined the walls, stacked nearly to the ceiling. Every flat surface was covered with stuff, stuff, and more stuff. Lotions and potions. Small, medium, and large boxes. Stacks of papers. Plastic shopping bags filled with more stuff. And clothing everywhere—on the bed, on the chair, on the floor. A narrow path led from the door to the bed, which had just enough clear space for Fiona to sleep. A little nest for herself amid the clutter.

I had seen this before. My aunt was a hoarder. No question.

Fiona swept her hands in the air, swirling her arms around her head. "It flew all over the room, flapping and squawking, back and forth."

I looked around. Nary a feather in sight, though there could have been a dozen feathers lost in the chaos of Fiona's bedroom.

She pointed to the window. "It perched up there for a second, so I jumped out of bed. I was going to shut the door to trap it in here, but it flew down to attack me. I ran downstairs, and it followed me." Her cadence slowed, her voice taking on a mystical quality as she looked off into the distance. "I opened the front door, and it swooped past me, disappearing into the darkness." She went quiet.

Incredibly detailed for a delusion.

I looked at the drapery rod above the bedroom window. I moved closer. There was a streak of something on the drape.

Greenish. Grayish. I touched a fingertip to it. It was dry. "Krissy, what does that look like to you?"

She squinched her eyes and peered at the spot. "Bird crap?"

"Could be."

Krissy hugged Fiona. "I'm sorry I didn't believe you, Ma. I'm sorry."

Fiona gave a harumph of satisfaction. "Maybe next time this family won't be so quick to dismiss me!"

She thanked me, said good night, and lay down on the accessible part of her bed. I felt a pang of sadness, seeing her curled there, imprisoned by her accumulated stuff.

Krissy and I headed downstairs. Harold was leaning against the kitchen counter, drinking a beer. "A crow? Seriously? You know how she gets."

Krissy said, "The crow pooped on the drapes in the bedroom."

Harold gave a grunt, took his beer, and went out to the camper. Didn't even say goodbye. That's just Harold.

As we drove back to the carriage house, Krissy asked, "How do you suppose that bird got into the house? Do you think Harold put it in there?"

I said, "The other explanation would be that a crow just happened to be flying around at night, and it just happened to find the back door standing open. And then decided it was a good idea to fly into the house. And then up the stairs to your mother's room. How likely is that?" I chuckled and then answered my own question. "About as likely as you winning big money at a casino and then finding a bag of bones in your trunk."

Kris said, "This is all weird, isn't it?"

I sighed. "Yes, it is. And I'm too tired to think."

Back at my place, I was asleep as soon as my head hit the pillow. Dreaming of black birds and dancing skeletons.

CHAPTER SEVENTEEN

Monday, November 24

I SLEPT RESTLESSLY, BUT WHEN I awoke, I sensed that a decision had been made somewhere in the night. Krissy could have Vince if that's what she wanted. She told me he hadn't called her since they got together. I could have reassured her that not calling was typical Vince, but I didn't. I let her take his silence as a personal rejection, if that's what she chose to do. Snotty, I know.

And as far as Nick was concerned, Bo Peep could keep him.

Decision: I was giving up on men.

Decision: I would be fine alone.

Decision: I was in control of my own destiny.

I felt extra-confident as I got dressed in my TriMak gear—long-sleeved navy-blue tee with the three circles logo, jeans, and my ASICS.

Downstairs on my couch, the blanket Kris had used was folded neatly on top of the pillow, and on top of that was a note from her: OUT 4 A WALK. BRB. At the bottom, in tiny print: URA DORK with a little smiley face.

I smiled as I fixed my breakfast—a healthy, confident meal for my new healthy, confident, man-free life. A bowl of cottage cheese mixed with Greek yogurt for extra protein, topped with chopped walnuts, a sprinkle of cinnamon, and a drizzle of honey.

My mother tells me often that my diet of Snickers, Almond Joys, and Milk Duds, washed down with Diet Coke, isn't the best. (I don't know about you, but when someone tells me I shouldn't, it makes me want to do it even more. But maybe that's just me.)

Of course, my broken heart tries to tell me that sugar is the answer to my sorrows, but Rational Me knows better. This morning's breakfast made Rational Me happy.

I watched the Monday morning news while standing at my kitchen sink as I finished eating. Local weather guy—sorry, meteorologist—Stuart Klump said we might get the first significant snow of the season later in the week. We'd had a few wet flakes earlier in the month. But the first "significant" snow meant roads would have to be plowed and sidewalks shoveled.

I washed my empty bowl and the spoon, dried them, and put them away. I wiped down the counter. Little-Bit-of-OCD Me likes to leave the place tidy when she heads to work.

As I turned off the TV, I asked Chloe, "Where did I pack my boots and gloves?" I could see the box in my mind. A plastic bin with a blue lid. Somewhere at Gram's since last winter. "Where's the box, Chloe? Is it in Gram's attic? Or the basement? Where did I put it? Huh, Kitty? Where?"

I swear cats can roll their eyes. She stood, stretched, and then high-tailed it out of the living room.

I called Krissy, got her location, and told her I'd pick her up on the way to TriMak. I put on my navy-blue, fleece-lined TriMak windbreaker and turned out the lights. When I opened the door, Chloe shot outside and disappeared through an opening under Gram's back porch.

I started Cricket, and Jimbo chirped a good morning as the car warmed up. With Fiona's car repossessed, Krissy had parked the Oldsmobile in her mom's garage. Krissy might have been able to borrow Gram's Buick, but it was in the shop getting repairs. Since Krissy had no money to rent a car, I'd told her I'd chauffeur her around.

She'd clapped her hands. "Oh, goody! I'll be your deputy!" She'd saluted me.

Oh boy.

Rational Me reminded me that this was a good thing, since the casino people might be looking for the car she'd driven from Lost Creek. Safer for Krissy this way.

Rational Me whispered, *What a nice cousin you are.* Jimbo chirped agreement as I headed toward Oak Street.

A couple blocks from home, I thought I caught a glimpse of the red truck again, turning the corner a block ahead of me. Snarky Me scoffed. *You're getting delusional like Fiona, imagining things.*

Krissy was waiting at the corner of Oak and Fifth, wearing black jeans with rips and buckles down the right leg and a bunch of zippers circling the left leg. She had Nathan's bomber jacket zipped up to her chin. Pink socks poked out above her black combat boots. She was hugging herself and shifting from foot to foot, trying to keep warm.

She ran to the car and jumped in. "Nippy out here. Where are we headed now? I could use some breakfast."

We swung through Burger Barn, and Krissy got three sausage-and-egg breakfast biscuits and a large coffee. My treat, just like everything else.

As we drove, Krissy asked between mouthfuls, "How did you end up in this job?"

I explained how I had worked as Trip's administrative assistant in the past, in a financial services company his father, Big George Kipling, owned. Big George fired his son one day, and that meant Trip had to fire me. Trip decided to start his own business—a detective agency—and invited me to join him as office manager. I'd recently gotten my official investigator's license and handed off my manager duties to someone else. "The company is called TriMak, after the two of us. Trip and Mack."

She said, "Okay, that is way cool. You're such a badass."

I told her how I'd been called an "impressive badass" in the past.

She washed the biscuit down with coffee, then asked, "Mack, are you ever scared?"

I wanted to tell her that I was never scared, always brave. But that would have been a big fat lie. "Of course I get scared," I said. "Who wouldn't be scared being attacked? Or threatened? Like your mom is right now. She has every right to be scared, not knowing who is doing this to her."

Krissy said, "If I had your job, I'd be worried every single day that someone was going to come after me. You see that on TV all the time. Someone you sent to jail gets out and comes after you. Or your family. Lots of psychos out there."

"Not so many of those around Three Rivers," I said. I didn't go into detail about everything I'd endured during my short tenure as an investigator. How I'd almost been shot, almost burned in my apartment, and then in a cornfield. Almost drowned in a urinal. I'd been choked, hit with a brick, and attacked with a crockpot. I'd come close to having my skull cracked with a hatchet, almost been tossed off a cliff, and I'd been at the business end of a gun barrel. And most recently, poked with a pitchfork and nearly drowned in a cistern.

I didn't mention that I'd survived all that while solving several cases in the last few months—and doing so brilliantly, if I do say so myself. All I said was, "I've had plenty of encounters with unstable people protecting themselves and their secrets, and they see me as getting in the way of that. It's all just part of the job." I sounded a lot braver than I felt.

"Well, like I said, you're a badass, cousin."

I tried to look modest. "I just love solving the puzzles. Every case is like a real-life game of Clue. And I get to play it every day."

The TriMak office is in a storefront on River Street with apartments upstairs. I parked in back on the concrete parking pad.

Waiting at the back door was Moe, the wrinkly, drooly mix of Shar-pei and pit bull who loves me. As in L-O-V-E love.

Moe and his dog-pals, Larry and Curly, belong to Ralph, the elderly man who rents one of the apartments above TriMak. The dogs are delighted, I'm sure, that their pack-leader, Ralph, is back home after recovering from a broken hip.

Moe followed us inside to the office kitchenette, where I got him a liver-flavored dog treat from the cupboard. Like I said, Moe loves me. He thinks I smell like liver.

I held my hand flat with the treat on my palm in front of Moe's face. "Wait . . . wait . . ." I told him. Drool poured from his mouth, but he waited, just the way I'd taught him. When I figured he couldn't wait a second longer, I said, "Take it!" and he slobbered the treat off my hand. "Good boy!" I said, and he wagged his whole body.

I went to the sink and washed off the drool just as Germany Jones came into the kitchenette. In his early twenties—tall and on the thin side—Germany looked professional in his TriMak shirt and jeans this morning, though his thick mop of curly brown hair remained untamed, as usual. I introduced him to Krissy.

She said, "Germany? Cool name."

While I used the one-cupper to brew coffee for Krissy and another for myself, Germany explained how he was conceived at Ramstein Air Force Base, and that's how he got the name. "My sister's name is Okinawa. You can guess why." They laughed together.

We took our coffees, and I gave Krissy a tour of TriMak. I pointed to the office on our left. The door was closed. "This is Chief Bronson's office. And that one next to it is, uh . . ." The words stuck in my throat. I swallowed hard and said, quickly, "Somebody else's." I hurried forward and pointed to the front office. "And this office is Trip's."

We'd reached the reception area. Germany was at his desk, working on his laptop. I said, "And this is command central, where Germany runs the place."

He smiled and gave me a salute. "Thanks, Wonder Chick."

Krissy said, "Who?"

Germany laughed. "She's Wonder Chick, and I'm her sidekick, Foghorn—like that cartoon rooster, you know? Superheroes, making the world safe for democracy. Don't tell anyone, please." He winked at her.

Krissy laughed. "Your secret's safe with me."

In front of the big window facing River Street, pieces of

a fake Christmas tree were strewn across the floor. Germany pointed at the tree and said, "I'm working on that today. Trip had it at the house."

I looked at Kris. "Maybe you could help him with that later, Krissy?" She agreed. Germany seemed grateful for the help, and I was grateful that Krissy wouldn't be following me around all day.

Everybody was happy. *Middle child. Peacemaker. C'est moi.*

I took Krissy to my office. Did I say office? Broom closet is the technical term. Krissy waited in the doorway of the former storeroom while I flicked on the overhead light. The bare bulb in the ceiling came on, and I walked to the desk in the corner, where I turned on the desk lamp.

On my desk was a tiny fake pine tree with little plastic snowflakes dangling from it. I called out to the lobby. "Thanks for the tree, Germany!"

"You're welcome!" he hollered back.

I sat at the desk, and Krissy took the folding chair I keep next to the desk for visitors. She looked around at the orange extension cord running from the ceiling fixture to the power strip on the desk where I plug in my laptop. She took in the Wonder Woman poster and the metal sculpture of the fierce little chicken on the desk.

"Nice digs," she said with a chuckle. "I expected something, uh, I don't know . . ."

"Bigger? Fancier?"

"Cleaner." She drew an index finger through the dust on the desk.

I scraped the dust off the end of the desk with my palm, then brushed my hands together over the wastebasket. "It's temporary. Just temporary," I said. I didn't want to get into the whole story of how hot-shot, former-big-city-cop, PI Sheena Shay came to TriMak and took the middle office across the hall. The office that was supposed to be mine. I was sick of whining about the whole deal, and for now, I was making peace with working out of the former broom closet. For now. *Just* for now.

I opened my laptop and started a file, as I always do with a new case. I talked out loud as I typed.

"Okay, Krissy. We have a lot going on here." I titled the case: BONES. "First, the bones. Who do they belong to, and how did the bones end up in that car you got from Delroy Bean?"

"Next case." I typed MONEY.

Kris said, "Yeah, Slade and Jacko. I met them and bam—they stole my suitcase and a bunch of my money. *And* they took off when they saw us. *And* they dumped the suitcase outside the motel where they stayed." She squirmed in the folding chair. "This is so exciting. Just like on TV."

I said, "I'll ask the chief if he can trace their license plate and find out who they are, where they came from. The last case is your mother." I typed FIONA. "What do we have so far?"

"Someone is harassing her. She owes money all over town, so it could be anyone."

I made notes to talk with Fiona's neighbors, the loan guy, and to dig into this business of Harold's. I finished my notes as we finished our coffee. "Is that it? Do we have everything?"

Krissy said, "I need to go back to my apartment in Lost Creek and get the rest of my stuff."

I said, "And I'd like to check out this casino."

Krissy said, "I want to come to the casino with you."

"Too risky. Someone will recognize you." I thought a moment. "The chief works undercover sometimes. In disguise.

We can ask him to help us. If you think of anything else, we can add it to the list."

She clapped her hands. "Okay, where do we start, Detective Prentice?"

"We talk to the chief."

CHAPTER EIGHTEEN

THE CHIEF'S DOOR WAS open, and he was at his desk. I rapped. He looked up. "Come on in, Chickie."

I introduced Krissy. The chief stood and shook her hand. "Nice to meet—" He stopped. "Wait. I remember you."

We took the two chairs in front of his desk, and the chief leaned back and smiled. "Kristen Fairchild, right? I remember you being at a party with some older kids at Rawley Park. Past curfew. Underaged drinking, as I recall." The chief was still an officer back then, twenty years ago.

Krissy's cheeks pinked. "Wow. You've got a great memory. Yes, I was just a sophomore, and they were a bunch of seniors. I was mad at you for spoiling our fun, but since the rest of them spent the night in jail, I figured I got off easy. Thanks for driving me home that night."

"You were a bit of a wild child, weren't you? Making, shall we say, less than wise choices? But I knew your home situation. We had a lot of calls from that house. Domestic disturbance calls."

Krissy gave an eye roll. "Ha! You mean knock-down, drag-out fights. Usually with my mother drinking and then getting mad at my dad. Throwing things, breaking stuff. She was a mean drunk."

He nodded. "I remember."

Krissy said, "But she's mellowed out now. Still has a temper, but she doesn't break things anymore. She just takes other people's—"

She stopped abruptly when she saw the cautioning look on my face. No need to talk to the chief about the money yet. Krissy got the message and said, "My mother is doing the best she can these days."

The chief smiled. "Glad to hear that. Your dad was a good man, and you were just a kid caught in the middle. I didn't want you to end up in juvie because your parents couldn't figure things out."

Krissy looked down at the floor. "Thank you, Chief. I appreciate how you handled everything back there."

He cleared his throat. "You're welcome. Sometimes you have to go with your gut and ignore the rule book." He frowned at me. "You can do that once you've had years of experience. Understand, Mack? For now, you be sure to follow the rules."

I nodded agreement. Anxious Me, Rational Me, and Little-Bit-of-OCD Me all love rules. But Badass Me often has opinions of her own.

The chief leaned forward and smiled at us. "Now what kind of trouble are you two in today?"

I said, "Not us—my aunt Fiona. Krissy's mother. She's gotten weird phone calls. Someone left a pile of dog poop on her steps, then a dead bird on the porch. And hung a noose in her plum tree."

Kris said, "Don't forget about the crow." She retold Fiona's story.

The chief scowled. "Sounds like kid pranks."

"Maybe, yes, the dog doodoo and birds, maybe the noose. But the phone calls? Who does that these days?"

Kris jumped in. "She doesn't have caller ID. She's living in the Stone Age."

The chief suppressed a smile. "I grew up in the Stone Age. Simpler times and in some ways, better."

Krissy blushed. "No offense, Chief Bronson."

He said, "None taken." He looked at me. "Any ideas who is doing the harassing?"

I shook my head. "I'll talk to her neighbors. She, uh, hasn't always gotten along well with everybody." Understatement.

The chief stood. We were done. "Keep me posted. Let me know if I can help."

I walked Krissy out to the front and left her talking to Germany. Then I circled back to the chief's office, went in, and closed the door. "One more thing, Chief."

I sat down and told him about the bones.

He leaned back in his chair and frowned. "You have a legal obligation to report finding a body, and to do it right away. You could be in trouble for concealing a corpse."

"It wasn't a body, actually. Just a burlap bag full of bones. And I didn't find it. Kris did. In the trunk of her car."

He asked, "You sure the bones are human?"

"Most definitely human. The skull was a human skull, with a big hole in the back of it. It was staring up at me . . ." I shivered. "Creepy."

"Okay, how did the bones end up in her car? How do you know she didn't kill the, uh, person?"

Krissy couldn't possibly be a murderer. Or could she? I hated myself for even wondering. "No, no, no," I said. "Krissy didn't kill anybody. Whoever those bones belong to has been dead a long time."

"But your cousin has been out of town how long? Do you know for sure where she's been, what she's been doing? Maybe she killed whoever it is and buried the body. Then dug it up again for some reason—maybe afraid it was going to be discovered. Then she stuck the bones in the bag, brought it here, and is just pretending she has no idea who it is or what happened. Maybe she's actually guilty and counting on you to help her figure out what to do next."

I felt hot. "You're trying to make my cousin into a murderer!"

He spat back. "Hey, cool your jets, Prentice. I'm just spitballin' here, spinning out theories. That's what *real* professionals do, trying to figure all the angles."

I hated how he emphasized the word "real." My fists balled in my lap, I looked at the floor, wrangling my emotions into submission.

The chief gave me another minute, then broke the silence. "Let's think this through. You're saying your cousin just happened to end up with this body—these bones—in the trunk of her car."

"Not actually her car," I said. "She got it from a garage."

He said, "Well, that's what she told you anyway. You have any proof of that?"

I didn't have any proof—just Krissy's word that she'd swapped cars with Delroy Bean. "I believe my cousin."

"I get it. You want to believe her. If it were my family, I'd feel the same way, but—"

I jumped in with what I figured the chief was about to

say next. "But we don't go with our feelings. We go with the evidence."

He nodded. "That's right."

"So I need evidence."

He pointed an index finger at me. "Bingo."

I said, "Okay. I'll go to Lost Creek and talk to the guy who gave her the car. Meanwhile, what about the bones?"

He said, "No options there. Give the bones to me, and I'll take them to the medical examiner. In my experience, it takes time—weeks or longer—to identify a body from old bones. That's assuming the person is even in the system. But the M.E. owes me one, so I'll see what we can do."

I told the chief we'd bring the bones to him right away and got up to leave. I didn't say anything about the casino money. I just hoped I wouldn't regret that.

CHAPTER NINETEEN

WE MADE A QUICK trip back to Gram's. I retrieved the bag of bones from the basement and brought it to Chief Bronson. Then I told Krissy I wanted to go talk to the guy at E-Z MONEY about Fiona's loan. She insisted on coming with me.

As we drove, she chattered away about how exciting it was to be my deputy. "I need a good deputy name. If you're Wonder Chickie and Germany is Foghorn, who should I be?"

"Crazy Krissy is a good fit."

"Shut up, Dork!"

I drove south from River Street past the area of town known as The Bottoms, past the abandoned paper factory. The factory and the neighborhood had once teemed with life. The massive red brick facility had become home to wildlife and squatters until recently, when a local real estate consortium bought the property and started renovations. The exterior of the building was half-painted with a bright, urban-looking mural. Elongated figures of buildings in black and white stood silhouetted against a background of deep reds, vibrant blues, and glowing chartreuse.

Kris said, "Looks like the old factory is getting a new life, huh?"

I filled her in on what I knew. "Lofts and offices. Big city stuff. That mural has gotten a lot of blowback. Folks think it's a little too city-fied for Three Rivers. But you can't stop progress."

Kris said, "It's happening everywhere. Back in Lost Creek, the town was basically dead. But lately, developers started gobbling up farmland for new subdivisions. Bedroom communities for Delport workers who are tired of the city."

I drove south past the new home improvement store—Builders' Central—that had opened the previous year. It was next to Milcross Builders, the family business that Nick's grandfather started decades ago. Nick and his dad run the business now.

I sighed. Nick-who-could-have-been-mine. If I hadn't been so stupid. Now it was too late. He was with someone else. And Vince had hooked up with Krissy. I needed to let go of both those situations, or I'd make myself crazy.

Where was my earlier confidence that I'd be fine alone? Rational Me cut off that line of thinking. *You're going to depress yourself. Focus!*

We reached the strip mall near the highway on the south end of Three Rivers, where my high school classmate Ronny has his snake store, sandwiched between Hair Galore and Magic Massage. A new tattoo place called SKINT had opened at the end of the strip.

"Ooh, I should get another tattoo," Krissy said, and then went on to describe exactly what she wanted. "What do you think, Mack?"

I'd been so focused on finding Wally Klemish's business that I hadn't heard a word. "Yeah, sounds good," I said.

Past the west end of the strip mall, set back from the highway, we found the block building with a big sign on top. E-Z MONEY. PAYDAY LOANS. GREAT RATES. An iron security grate covered the large front window of the dark green building. A similar grate protected the glass in the front door. Cash business equals extra security.

I parked Cricket. "You should probably wait in the car," I told Krissy.

"No way! I want to see this scum-sucking—"

I cut her off. "We don't have any proof that he's been harassing your mother. We're just here to ask questions."

Krissy huffed. "He lent my mother money. He's a blood-sucking vampire who preys on desperate people. I want to see his face and punch him!"

"You are definitely not coming in with that attitude. We don't know who this guy is, or what's going on, so you have to let me handle this. Understand?"

She grumbled a protest, then nodded.

The front door of the place hadn't been cleaned in ages. The entryway smelled of stale cigarette smoke and desperation. A mismatched pair of chairs—one overstuffed with cracked fake leather upholstery and the other a generic office conference room chair—were the only furnishings in the small waiting area. Wally Klemish didn't want his customers to get too comfortable.

A chest-high counter topped with a filthy glass partition separated the waiting space from the back of the place. Krissy wiped her index finger down the glass, then held the black tip toward me. She whispered, "Just like home."

I crinkled my nose. On the counter, a small bell—like a doorbell—sat with a sign that read RING FOR SERVICE.

I rang and heard a buzzing in the back of the building. We waited. Nobody came.

I buzzed again, and after a minute, a toilet flushed somewhere in the back. Another minute later, an enormous man, whose frame filled the entire hallway, came out from the back of the office, breathing hard as he buckled his belt.

He hollered. "Give me a sec! I was in the can." He looked up, saw me, and turned red. "Jesus, you're not him."

I smiled. "No, I'm not him, whoever he is."

He frowned as he looked me up and down. "You don't look like you need a loan."

I took that as a compliment. "Are you Wally?"

"Who's asking?" He frowned deeper.

I hadn't thought this through. This guy was a loan shark, a predator—someone who could make trouble for me and was maybe already making trouble for Fiona. I'd strolled in here unprepared. *Nice going, Sherlock. Now what?*

Anxious Me started to panic. *Oh my God! He's huge! He's going to break our kneecaps!*

I decided to play it straight. "You know my aunt, Fiona Fairchild."

He narrowed his eyes and frowned. "Don't recall the name."

Krissy gave a low growl and said, "She owes you money. She told me so."

He shook his head. "Nope. Not ringin' any bells. And even if it did, there's confidentiality between us loaners and our loanees in this business."

Rational Me, a real stickler for good grammar, wanted to explain the proper use of *loan* versus *lend.* But Anxious Me is an even bigger stickler for not pissing big guys off, so I said nothing.

Wally restated his claim. "Nope, never heard of any broad called—what was it you said? Florence something?"

I sensed Krissy tense behind me. I stepped back, forcing her to retreat. I hissed over my shoulder, "Let me handle this."

Wally said, "Unless you need a loan, you gotta leave. I need to lock up. I've got somewhere to be." He came out from behind the partition. He seemed even more massive close up.

"You got a hot date?" Krissy snarled.

Wally glared at her. "You getting' smart? Huh? Are you?"

Anxious Me freaked out a little. *Make her shut up. She's gonna get us killed.*

Krissy stepped around me, fists up.

Anxious Me freaked more. *OMG, she's gonna hit him.* He had a hundred pounds on her. This was not going to end well.

Wally took a moment, looked Krissy up and down, then gave a nasty laugh. "Ha! I don't hit girls. Even bitchy ones." He came forward fast and, with his bulk, herded us toward the door.

I didn't need any encouragement. With a loud snap, the door locked behind us. Krissy made a move as if she was going back, but I pulled her away from the building.

Back in the car, I forced my breath to slow. "That was stupid, Kris. He could have pulverized you."

She gave a huff. "At least we made it clear—we see what he's doing, and he'd better watch out. Now he knows we know."

I asked, as I started Cricket, "And what exactly do you think we know?"

Krissy grunted. "That he's been pressuring my mother to repay the loan."

I said, "We don't know that. He said he never heard of Fiona."

"And you believe him?"

I said, "Until we have proof to the contrary, yes." *Investigations 101: You know when you know. Everything else is just guessing.*

Kris said, "He'd better watch his back."

"You realize that's the same message he gave us?" I shook off a wave of apprehension as I turned Cricket toward Fiona's house. "I need to talk to your mother. I'll drop you at TriMak. You're helping Germany with the tree, right?" I didn't want Krissy to blow up at Fiona again.

"Fine with me. I don't want to see her. Not now. Not ever."

I left Krissy at TriMak with Germany, brainstorming nicknames for herself as a second sidekick for Wonder Chick. Kris said, "What about Wildwing?"

As I walked away, Germany suggested "Flighty." I chuckled all the way out to the car.

Flighty. That's so Kris.

CHAPTER TWENTY

FIONA LOOKED UP FROM the kitchen table when I knocked on the window in her back door. She waved me in. She was at the table with a Bloody Mary and a bologna sandwich.

I glanced at the kitchen wall clock.

Fiona noticed. "Don't judge. It's past noon."

I smiled. "No judgment here, Fiona. I've had my own issues."

She held up the glass. "You want one?"

"No thanks. I just came from E-Z MONEY. Wally Klemish says he doesn't know you."

Fiona glared. "That's bullshit!"

I gave a shrug as I sat down at the table. "Maybe he's got so many customers he just didn't remember you."

"Bull. I had to put up my car because I don't have a job. He has the car now, so he knows damn well who I am."

I said, "He's a really big guy. Have you seen him around your house?"

"No, I haven't seen him since I got the loan. But his partner was here once."

"Who is his partner?"

"A woman named, uh, let me think. Starts with a P. No, it starts with R. Oh, I don't remember. But she's about your age, and she's tall. Not as tall as Kristen, but tall."

"Hair color? Eye color? Tattoos? Scars?" Who was this woman, and what did she do for Wally? I figured she wasn't a kneecap basher. That's no job for a woman.

"When she came over to talk to me, she was dressed real nice. No tattoos. Looked like a lawyer."

"Maybe she *is* a lawyer?"

"She left her card here." Fiona went to her cluttered desk in the next room. From the doorway, I watched her plow through the piles of papers covering it. A moment later, she straightened, holding up a business card. "Aha!" she said, flashing a triumphant grin, as if she'd just pulled off a magic trick.

Magic, indeed—finding anything in a mess like Fiona's.

I read it aloud: "'E-Z MONEY Laureen Page, Representative.' I'll give Ms. Page a call and see what she has to say."

Fiona gave me one of her angelic smiles and gushed, "Thank you, thank you, thank you. I honestly don't know what I would have done without you and Kristen. You're saving me." She'd no doubt learned early how to play the helpless card—batting her eyelashes to get her older siblings to do for her what she should've been doing for herself.

On the way back to TriMak, I called Laureen Page's number, got her voicemail, and asked her to call me back regarding "a pressing matter." She called back right away, her voice silky smooth. She told me she was meeting a client at Old Town Tap in fifteen minutes and could give me five minutes if I met her there. I didn't bother to tell Krissy. No need for her to make another scene, this time with Wally Klemish's business partner.

I was in a booth by the door when Laureen Page glided into the Tap. She looked as silky smooth as her voice. Tall, thin, and tan, she wore a sleek fitting suit in a soft gray, a crisp white blouse with a chunky gold necklace visible at the open collar.

The bar wasn't crowded—just three cops having a break at a nearby table. They checked her out. If she noticed them, she gave no indication of it. *Haughty. That's the word.*

I waved, and she came to the booth. We shook. She sat.

I'd ordered a Diet Coke. She declined my offer to buy her one. I slid my card across the table to her.

She looked at it. "What is it you want, Ms. Prentice?"

"Well, Ms. Page, it seems that you and my aunt Fiona have crossed paths."

She raised an eyebrow. "Fiona?" She looked up at the ceiling and then smiled. "Oh! Fiona Fairchild. Yes. Such a nice lady. It's a shame she found herself in that position."

"What position is that?"

"In financial straits. Needing our help."

I felt my jaw tighten. I leaned forward, throwing in air quotes as I made my point. "Your 'help' is rather predatory, isn't it? You take advantage of people when they are at their lowest. Tell me, Ms. Page—what kind of 'help' is that?"

She leaned back in the booth and gave me an indulgent smile. Then, in a tone as gentle as if she were speaking to a child, she said, "I understand how you feel, and I completely disagree."

My turn to lean back. "Okay, so enlighten me. How do you see it?"

She smiled again. Infinitely patient. Calm, confident, cool. "People need help, and we provide it. When nobody else is there for them, we are."

"Yeah, you're there, all right—there to take advantage of them when they're down and out." My jaw tightened again. "How very kind of you."

She leaned forward, elbows on the table, leaning her chin on her folded hands. "Tell me, Ms. Prentice, are you from a big family?"

"Yes, but what does that matter?"

"Who among your big family was willing to help your aunt? Who was willing to advance her the cash she needed?"

I felt my cheeks heat up and started to jump to the family's defense, but she lifted a hand to stop me. "Hear me out. My family was the same way. When my brother had troubles, everyone said he'd made his own bed and refused to help. That's when he decided to start the business. He knows what it's like to be desperate, unable to make rent, in danger of losing your job because you can't afford to repair your car."

So big Wally was Laureen's brother.

She continued. "As soon as he could, he started helping others in trouble. It's a noble cause. We meet a need. We help those who've fallen through the cracks."

I was starting to see her point, though I didn't want to. I wanted to stay judgmental, to hate on the E-Z Money crowd. "But you charge a ridiculous amount of interest, don't you? You have to acknowledge *that*."

"We see it as simply charging what the market will bear. People need help, and we provide it. True, there is no legal limit on what we can charge, but there is a limit on how much we can lend, so it balances out. In fact, we're tightly regulated by the state. Consumer protection regulations are strict. We follow the rules—to the letter."

"So, nothing outside the law? No intimidation tactics? No threats of harm?"

She stiffened. "Absolutely not!" She looked up. "My next appointment is here, so you'll have to excuse me. Please tell your aunt to call me if she needs to renegotiate her terms. I'll be happy to help her. Nice to meet you." We shook again, and I watched her glide toward the man waiting for her at the bar.

As she led the man toward a booth in the back of the Tap, the cops at the table watched her from behind. One waggled his eyebrows at his buddy, and all three of them laughed. *Boys. Boys. Boys.*

I left my unfinished soda and walked out. Laureen certainly wasn't the type to send messy messages with dog droppings, dead birds, and nooses. Her brother Wally, huge as he was, would've been noticed lurking about. I tentatively crossed both of them off my list of potential harassers.

The simple thing would be to install security cameras around Fiona's house. If we did that, I'd be footing the bill, since Fiona was broke, and I'd already told Krissy her illegal casino winnings were off limits.

It was time to talk with Fiona's neighbors—Mr. Rooney with the Rottweilers, and Mrs. McGruder with the chickens. Maybe they'd seen something or someone lurking about. Or maybe one of them was the lurker.

CHAPTER TWENTY-ONE

YOU KNOW HOW PEOPLE start to resemble their dogs? Well, Mrs. McGruder had started to resemble her chickens. A short, round woman who looked to be pushing seventy, she had wild, impossibly red hair that stood up in all directions, like a crown of feathers on the top of her head. Heavy-breasted and sway-backed, she strutted toward me like a giant chicken. In sensible shoes.

"Mrs. McGruder? I'm Mackenzie Prentice," I pointed to Fiona's house next door. "I'm Fiona's niece."

She gave a cluck, and the little wattle of fat under her chin wiggled. "You poor girl. That woman is the worst neighbor anyone could have. She hates my chickens. You know, she threatened to roast them for clucking. Chickens have to cluck, you know? The nerve! I'd like to roast her!"

I ignored that. "I'm sorry that she's given you any trouble." Taking the apologetic route. Fiona could probably do an apology tour around the whole town.

Mrs. McGruder scooped up a gray hen with mottled feathers and stroked it. "Your aunt is nothing but trouble. Did she tell you she tried to steal my husband? She's an awful person." She went on about the summer weeds in Fiona's yard and her failure to keep her sidewalk clear of snow in the winter. "Her sidewalk was so icy last winter, I almost broke my neck. She doesn't give a hoot about anyone but herself."

I bit my lip, shaking my head. The soul of empathy. "I don't know how you've resisted paying her back for all the trouble." *Leading the witness. Smooth, Prentice.* Rational Me nodded approval.

She gave me sly eyes. "No need for me to do that. That's what the authorities are for." She told me how she'd called the city about the weeds and the snow and ice. "They've warned her and warned her, but she's ignored everything. I imagine she owes a small fortune in fines. Honestly, I don't understand how anyone ignores the city regulations. When I decided to get my birds, I had to jump through a hundred hoops before they'd even let me have one chicken." She set the gray hen down and picked up a brown one. "It would be a better world if they paid more attention to who gets to have children these days. I swear, the brats in this neighborhood are the worst—harassing my girls, causing a ruckus."

"Harassing your girls?"

"Yes, kids come to the coop and get the birds all agitated. Makes it so stressful for them, they stop laying. They start pecking at each other." She set the brown hen down, grabbed a bag of chicken feed, and tossed handfuls to her flock. "This is their feed, but they eat whatever they find on the ground. Bugs, grubs, and especially crickets. They love the challenge of catching crickets."

At that moment, as if on cue, two of the hens spotted a juicy-looking beetle that had the misfortune to be crossing the hen yard. A fat hen with pink feet grabbed it first and gulped it down.

The second hen, furious about losing the snack, launched herself at the first one—pecking, flapping, and squawking with more violence than I ever would have expected from a chicken.

Mrs. McGruder took quick steps toward them, clapping her hands as she shouted, "Stop that, Cleopatra! Leave Judy alone!" The hens separated and sulked off to their neutral corners.

I laughed.

She explained. "I named them after famous women." She pointed. "Cleopatra is the one with the puffy crown of feathers, like a headdress. And that's Judy Garland over there, the one with the red feet. Like the ruby slippers."

I've never paid much—or actually any—attention to chicken feet. I stared at Judy Garland's claws. They had a little pinkish tint, but they were a far cry from red. Mrs. McGruder clearly had a better imagination than I have.

She pointed at a hen with blonde feathers and the biggest bosom in the group. "That's Marilyn," she said. Going for the obvious. "And over there is Oprah." A big brown hen. Another obvious choice. She pointed at a hen with orange feathers as it came closer to us. "And this is Lucille Ball."

Cleopatra, Judy Garland, Marilyn Monroe, Oprah, Lucille Ball. Quite the collection. My aunt said she hated the chickens, but I decided they were cute. Interesting, actually. And I could tell that Mrs. McGruder was really into raising them. I thought about my own two parakeets, Tweet and Chirp, who lived in Gram's front parlor. Cute birds, cute names. What's not to like?

I thanked Mrs. McGruder for her time and the education. She wasn't at all the "witch" Krissy said she was.

As I walked past the house, the back door opened and a girl about sixteen stepped out. Tall, with an athletic build, she was—no question—related to Mrs. McGruder. Her natural-looking red hair stuck out like feathers, and she walked toward us with the same kind of strut.

Mrs. McGruder introduced her. "My granddaughter, Marigold."

The girl gave me a weak smile.

"And Marigold," Mrs. McGruder added, "this is Mackenzie. Mrs. Fairchild next door is her aunt."

Marigold wrinkled up her nose and sneered. "We hate her."

Her grandmother said, "Now, Marigold, it's not nice to say things like that."

The girl crossed her arms and stuck out her lower lip. "I don't care. We hate her."

I lied and told Marigold it was nice to meet her. She ignored me and strutted across the yard to the chicken coop.

Petulant teenager. We remember those days, Rational Me said.

Snarky huffed. *Snotty little brat.*

I thanked Mrs. McGruder again for her time and the education. I walked away, reviewing the evidence I'd gathered. Mrs. McGruder had denied doing anything personally to Fiona, though she'd seemed tickled pink to use legal channels to get her in trouble. Would this woman throw a dead robin on a porch? She was more likely to give a dead bird a royal send-off. And I hadn't seen a dog, so no ready supply of dog droppings. Could she have hung the noose in the tree? Maybe. But she didn't seem angry enough—or agile enough—to go to all that trouble.

Maybe pouty Marigold was the poop-dropper and the dead bird depositor. She was tall enough and looked strong enough to be the noose hanger—but would she? Or maybe she had a brother or a boyfriend who'd do her dirty work for her.

Mental note: dig further.

I walked to Mr. Rooney's house on the opposite side of Fiona's. A chain-link fence surrounding the yard held BEWARE OF DOG signs in several places. I paused, rattling the metal gate as I cleared my throat loudly. I gave the loudest whistle I could muster. *Keep your enemies closer.* I just hoped that any dog intent on hurtling itself at me would do so while I was still outside the fence.

Nothing. I whistled again. Nothing again.

I unlatched the gate, walked up the porch steps, and knocked on the door. Nothing. I rang the bell and waited. No ferocious barking. No sounds at all from within. I moved to the window overlooking the porch, shaded my eyes, and peered into the house. No signs of life—just the pendulum swaying in the bottom of the grandfather clock against the living room wall. *Tick, tock. Tick, tock.*

I took out a business card and wrote a note on the back, asking Mr. Rooney to give me a call. I wedged it in the door jamb and went back to Cricket.

As I drove and the car warmed up, Jimbo started chirping like crazy. Maybe I smelled like the chickens, and he didn't want to end up as Judy Garland's lunch.

CHAPTER TWENTY-TWO

BEFORE HEADING BACK TO TriMak, I texted my police contact and sort-of friend Heather Sullivan, a detective with Three Rivers PD. She agreed to see me.

Heather had worked with—and slept with—my late ex-husband Billy, then got sober and made her amends to me. I'd forgiven her, and we have since developed a quasi-friendship and a sort of cooperative working relationship. Meaning I provide her with information sometimes, and she doesn't arrest me for interfering in police matters. Works for me.

Heather was in her office when I got there. She's about my age, but there the resemblance ends. She looked particularly good today with navy jacket and crisply creased navy slacks. Her periwinkle blue blouse did something extra sparkly to her blue eyes, and her long blonde hair was swept into a braided bun at the nape of her neck. Gram would say, "Neat as a pin," and I would have to agree.

Heather is gorgeous, but I know that under her image of

"polished professional female detective" beats a badass-don't-even-think-about-it cop's heart.

She sounded weary. "What can I do for you today, *Detective* Prentice?" She put a little sarcastic spin on the label.

I smiled and spun it right back. "Thanks for seeing me, *Detective* Sullivan. I'm here about my aunt, Fiona Fairchild."

"What about your aunt?"

"She's being harassed." I told her about the phone calls, the dog pile, the dead bird, and the noose.

Heather leaned back in her office chair, crossing her arms. "Good grief. You don't have anything more important to deal with than what sounds like a bunch of adolescent pranks?"

I suddenly felt like a complete dope. The chief had said pretty much the same thing. He and Heather were probably right. "The chief thinks that too."

She nodded. "So the two *actual* cops in your world think that's what it is. Why do you think it's anything else?"

I leaned forward. "Fiona's been involved with Wally Klemish at that E-Z MONEY business. Maybe he's been harassing her for failure to pay him back."

"I know that business. They don't need to threaten people. They have access to bank accounts—you sign up when they give you the money. If she doesn't pay, he takes her to court. Legit. Maybe taking advantage of people who are in a tough spot, but strictly legit. We had a few complaints in the past from people who didn't want to read the fine print, but the business operates completely inside the state regs. End of story." She paused. "Has your aunt thought about installing security cameras?"

"She won't do that."

"Okay, then, how about you do a stakeout tonight and see if you can catch the middle schooler who thinks it's hilarious to leave poop on porches?"

I gave her a little sneer. "Whatever," I said. She was no help at all, but the stakeout idea might be our only option. Worth a shot.

"One other thing," Heather said, leaning forward. "Since you're always snooping around town . . ."

I bristled. Was an insult coming?

She said, "I could use your, um, skills." She gave a little smile. "Specifically, your snooping skills."

My turn to sit back and smile. "My snooping skills. You're *asking* me to use my snooping skills. To help you. Is that right?" *And then she'll owe us. This is exciting.*

She raised an eyebrow. "Okay, don't get carried away. We've had a couple reports of phony twenty-dollar bills showing up in town. A federal agent was here earlier talking with Chief Wardell about it. Evidently part of a big deal case out of Chicago. Anyway, as long as you're out and about, I'd appreciate it if you let me know if you hear anything. While you're snooping into, um, other things. Whatever those might be. Which I do *not* want to know about."

My Spidey senses tingled. "Fake money? Where?"

"The Kwik Stop and Old Town Tap, so far."

Heather's laptop dinged, and she looked over at the screen as my stomach did a slow churn. *Had Krissy spent casino money in both those places? Was it possible?*

Spidey went DEFCON One. *Crap! Crap! Crappity crap! Illegal casino is one thing. Counterfeit money is a whole 'nother story.* Sweat beaded on my upper lip, and my cheeks went hot. I hoped Heather couldn't hear my heart pounding. I stood and tried to sound casual, despite the tightness in my throat. "Okay, I'll be sure to let you know if I hear anything."

She looked up, frowning. "See that you do." As if she were my boss. As if reporting to her was part of my job. *The nerve.*

I resisted saluting. *Yes, Detective Sullivan. I will do that.* Snarky added something I do not care to repeat.

I managed to walk out of the building before Anxious Me started sprinting to the car. I texted Krissy that we had to talk. She texted back that she and Germany had gone to Target to buy Christmas decorations for the office tree.

Lovely. Nero fiddling while Rome burns.

CHAPTER TWENTY-THREE

A BLACK CAR WITH US government plates was parked on the street in front of TriMak as I drove past. I parked in the back and went to my office. The chief came and got me. "Mack? You have a minute?"

I followed the chief to his office. A man in his forties with dark black hair and steel blue eyes sat in front of the desk. His black suit screamed government agent.

The chief said, "Mackenzie Prentice, this is Agent Sterling of the Secret Service."

The man in black handed me his card. The US Secret Service emblem was at the top. Then, "Department of Homeland Security. Garner Sterling, Special Agent. Criminal Investigations Division. Chicago."

I smiled. "Secret Service? Is the president in town?"

Sterling's smile—tight and fleeting—failed to reach his eyes. "A common misconception, Ms. Prentice. We do much more than provide protection. We enforce federal laws. In this case, counterfeiting."

My stomach dropped, then knotted. *What has Krissy gotten herself into?*

The chief said, "Chief Wardell over at the PD recommended Agent Sterling talk to us—"

Sterling held up a hand and looked at the chief. "I'll let you brief your operatives on this situation. The government appreciates your cooperation."

Agent Sterling stood. The chief stood. So did I. It seemed the thing to do.

Sterling nodded at me. "Ms. Prentice."

I resisted a sudden urge to curtsy.

Sterling nodded to the chief. "Mr. Bronson."

The chief stood taller. "We'll cooperate to the fullest, Agent Sterling. And it's *Chief* Bronson."

Sterling nodded again. "Of course. My apologies. Thank you, Chief Bronson."

Proper pecking order re-established, Sterling left.

I sat in the chair Agent Sterling had vacated. It was still warm. I looked at the chief. "What the heck was that about?"

"Chief Wardell sent him over here. Figured we might be able to help, since we're the only agency in town."

"But a federal case? Counterfeiting?" I told the chief about the rumor my mother had heard about the feds investigating an illegal casino. I left out the part about Krissy and the money she'd won.

Chief Bronson said, "That could be it. Sterling thinks there may be a connection with the syndicate out of Chicago."

I swallowed. "Syndicate? As in organized crime?"

"That's what Sterling said. Money laundering. Funneling counterfeit currency into the system."

The knot in my stomach got tighter. I felt like throwing

up. Krissy won mob money. Counterfeit mob money. And they were going to want their money back. *Oh geez. Krissy and trouble, still together after all these years.*

The chief was talking. "So keep your ears open, okay? Let me know if you hear anything."

I told the chief I had somewhere I needed to be and promised to keep him informed. I got up fast and headed for the door.

"Be careful, Chickie," he called after me. "Don't go rushing into anything. If the feds are involved, it's a big-time operation. You don't want to be caught in the crossfire."

I stopped and turned. My voice came out higher than usual. "Crossfire? Like a shootout?" Images from old gangster movies flashed—machine guns spraying, bodies flying.

He said, "You never know what people are going to do when they're cornered. Just be careful, okay?"

Endearing how the chief looks out for me. Endearing, yes—and terrifying to think about the reasons he might need to.

CHAPTER TWENTY-FOUR

KRISSY AND GERMANY CAME back from Target. I yanked her into my office, closed the door, and sat her in the folding chair. "Krissy, think hard right now. You paid for shots and burgers the other night at the Tap. And you told me you'd gotten gas at the Kwik Stop. How did you pay for that stuff?"

She paused, squinting at the ceiling. "Let me think. Okay, yeah, I bought gum and a Snickers and gas at the Kwik Stop—"

I cut her off. "Krissy! Focus! How did you *pay* for that stuff?"

She looked at me and gave a huff. "I paid cash."

"Casino money?"

"Well, yeah. Twenties from the casino. Why are you asking?"

"The chief and I just had a visit from a federal agent." I filled her in.

She went pale and sucked in a breath. "Holy crap. Do you think all the money is fake?"

I said, "I'm not sure. Bottom line is, we have to tell the chief." I knew Krissy should tell the authorities all she knew. But I was terrified what the counterfeiters—mobsters—might do if they found out she'd snitched. And they would find out because those people have eyes and ears everywhere.

Anxious Me flashed forward, Krissy falling under a hail of machine gun bullets. The gun in the hands of some thug with big shoulders and a fedora, sounding like Jimmy Cagney as he shouted, "That's what you get, see? You shouldn't have messed with us, see?"

Rational Me said, *You watch too many old movies.* No argument there.

Krissy's cell phone dinged. She read the text. "It's Jared. He wants to meet at Werner's Market." She looked up, wide-eyed. "He said it's life or death. I'm scared, Mackenzie. What should I do?"

I knew that the best and wisest choice in that moment would have been to go to the chief. But I don't always make the wisest choices. Curiosity trumped caution. "Let's go to Werner's."

Werner's Market is a half hour east of Three Rivers, on the way to Lost Creek. It's one of those farm-to-table stores run by the Mennonites. It's always busy, so it's a good choice for a public meeting.

Werner's parking lot was full, as usual, with pickup trucks, a couple of Amish buggies, and assorted cars. We parked Cricket toward the front, near the long, covered porch. We had a good view of the people coming and going.

To the left, several pieces of outdoor furniture were on display. My uncle had bought a glider here for Gram's front porch several years ago. That glider is one of my favorite thinking spots, with its view to Gram's massive hydrangea bushes surrounding the porch.

This time of year, just before Thanksgiving, fall decorations were in abundance. Tied bundles of cornstalks lined the wall behind wicker baskets filled with bundles of colorful dried corncobs. Rustic-looking carved wooden signs—the kind you hang by the front door—read WELCOME and AUTUMN GREETINGS and HAPPY HARVEST. I knew that in another week or so, all of this autumn decor would be replaced with Christmas decorations.

The porch held a gathering of metal-sculpted animals. Cats, dogs, and birds of various sizes stood in line with small, medium, and large metal flamingoes. Whimsical, colorful, and creative. Especially the flock of metal chickens—all sizes, all colors—almost as interesting as Mrs. McGruder's.

An adult-sized scarecrow at the end of the porch held a basket with a bunch of little scarecrows attached to wooden dowels. Gram sticks things like that in her flowerpots on the porch after the summer flowers have faded.

I personally will never own a scarecrow in any form, not even a tiny one. Not after one tried to kill me in a recent case. But I thought about picking one up for Gram for Christmas, then remembered we were at Werner's on business.

Cars streamed into the parking lot, and people streamed into the store. I glanced at Krissy as she fidgeted in the passenger's seat, scanning every car, every shopper. "Where the hell is he?" Her voice was tight, the words clipped. Then she bolted upright, pointing. "There he is!" She reached for the door handle, ready to jump out and give chase.

I grabbed her arm. "Wait until he's inside."

Jared was a short guy in his early to mid-forties, with a couple days' growth of beard, wearing an oversized Green Bay Packers jersey over dark blue sweatpants. He pulled his baseball cap low over his brow as he followed a group of women into the market.

We waited a minute, then followed him inside. We feigned interest in various displays until I spotted the jersey in a back corner of the store, where Jared was studying a pile of pumpkins.

Krissy approached. "Hey, Jared."

He startled and then turned, a look of wild desperation on his face.

Krissy said, "This is my cousin Mackenzie. She's a detective and she's helping me out. My mother—"

He held up a hand. "I don't care. I just need you to give the money back."

Krissy shrugged. "I don't have it."

He paled. "What do you mean you don't have it?"

"Well, I have some of it but not all of it. I'm trying to tell you that my mother—"

He stopped her again. "Marcus is pissed, and he told me I have twenty-four hours to get that money, or I'm a dead man." He looked around, his face draining of color as he started sweating profusely. He pulled at the front of his jersey, stretching the fabric away from his neck, sucking in big breaths.

I stepped toward him, got in his face. "What do you know about the counterfeiting?"

He got even paler as he took a step back, fell and sat, hard, on a big pumpkin. He put his head in his hands, muttering, "Jesus. Oh, Jesus. I'm a dead man. I'm a dead man." Then he looked up at Krissy. "You have to give me whatever money you have left. These guys are not messing around. It's not just Marcus. These are guys from Chicago. *Business*men. Get it?"

"Gangsters?" Krissy looked as pale as Jared.

Jared's voice went up an octave. "Gangsters. Mobsters. Wise guys. Thugs. Call them whatever you want. They're bad people, Kris. They're threatening to hurt me—really hurt me—if they don't get the money back. And they'll hurt you too."

I looked around, nervous at the thought that these guys, whoever they were, had followed Jared here and were watching us. But I saw only women in calico dresses and other average-looking shoppers.

Jared started hyperventilating, his breath coming in rasping bursts, sweat pouring off his forehead. I grabbed a plastic produce bag from the holder by the apple display, opened it, and handed it to Jared. "Breathe into this," I said, crouching beside him.

He closed his eyes and breathed in and out a few times in the bag. His breath calmed. He opened his eyes, looked up, and gave a little strangled sound.

I turned and looked up at Danny DeVito. Well, not him, of course, but a man who might have been his stunt double. About five foot six, with thinning black hair and a heavy five o'clock shadow. His arms looked too long for his torso, his legs too short. His expansive girth protruded over his belt.

He gave Krissy a nasty grin. "We meet again," he said.

I helped Jared to his feet. He pointed at Kris as he blurted, "Marcus! I was just asking her where the money is."

Krissy rushed to say, "And I don't have it. My mother—"

Marcus gave a scowl. "I don't give a rat's ass about your mother," he said and turned to me. "I don't know you, do I?"

I reached to shake hands. He took my hand reluctantly. I said, "Detective Mack Prentice."

He quickly let go, shrinking back a little. "A cop?"

Krissy started to correct him, but I held up a finger to silence her. I nodded. "Yes, that's right."

Marcus gave me a long look, then a tight smile. His teeth looked too big for his mouth. "No reason to involve law enforcement here, Detective. This is simply a small family matter." He gave a little chuckle. "A little misunderstanding, isn't that right, Jared?"

Jared nodded, mute.

Marcus said, "That's right. And Jared, I'm confident you'll give me a satisfactory answer by the end of today."

Jared nodded vigorously. "Yes, sir. I will, sir."

Marcus Grubb turned quickly, wound his way back through the crowd and left the store.

Krissy turned to Jared, fuming. She grabbed him by his jersey. "You told him I'd be meeting you here? How could you!"

Jared grabbed her wrists with both hands. "He threatened to do things to me if I didn't call you. Bad, bad things." He looked ready to cry.

Krissy let him go, then turned to me. "What do we do now?"

I waited a beat, thinking, then said, "Well, one good thing is that this Marcus guy thinks I'm a cop. We'll continue to let him think that."

Krissy gave me wide eyes. "What *are* we going to do, Mack? He thinks I have the money, and I only have a little left. My mother lost the rest gambling. And if it *is* counterfeit, and the government is investigating, I have to warn my friend Charlene."

I said, "We need leverage. Evidence that will persuade this Marcus to back off and call off his goons. But the feds are already involved, and we don't want to get in their way." I could imagine the scolding I'd get from the chief. He got upset enough if I got in the way of local Three Rivers police operations.

Krissy was adamant. "I'm going to Lost Creek to warn Charlene. And I have to get the rest of my stuff from the apartment."

I said, "Okay. I want to check out the casino, maybe figure out if Slade and Jacko are connected to it. But, Kris, it's too dangerous for you to be seen there. Let's go back to TriMak and ask the chief to help us out."

We left Jared in the pumpkins and headed back to Three Rivers. I spun my theories in the car. "My guess is Marcus Grubb and his mob friends are mixing the fakes in with real twenties. Here and there, so as not to arouse suspicion. And probably not giving any fakes to the locals who gamble there."

"And Robert gave them to me by mistake?"

"Yep, that's my guess. They probably just give them to out-of-towners, who will take the fakes away and not realize what's going on. Could be passing them in the surrounding states."

Krissy said, "A lot of tourists come through that area. People heading for resorts farther north or into Canada."

I said, "And taking the funny money with them."

"Just like I did," she said. "Oh man, oh man." She was uncharacteristically quiet on the rest of the drive.

When we got to TriMak, Chief Bronson was in the kitchen making himself a peanut butter sandwich. I told him Krissy needed to go back to Lost Creek but didn't want to be recognized.

Before he could ask for details, Krissy piped up. "I had some trouble back there. Mack told me you work undercover sometimes, and I wonder if you could fix me up with a disguise?"

Chief Bronson frowned. "What kind of trouble are we talking about?"

I jumped in before Krissy could be too honest. I hated to tell the chief a fib, but I didn't want to tell him everything. I didn't want him warning me to stay out of trouble. I wanted to figure this whole thing out and get whatever evidence I could find—evidence that the casino was involved in counterfeiting. Maybe figure out what happened to the guy whose bones we'd found. I wanted to be able to report "case solved" to the chief. I wanted to see that look of pride on his face when he said, "Well done, Chickie."

So, I lied.

I told him, "It's just a disagreement among friends, Chief. But Krissy doesn't want to take the chance someone will recognize her. We just need to get into her old apartment, grab her stuff, and get out. Quick trip."

The chief frowned, scrutinizing me. I gave a shrug, trying to look as innocent and ignorant as possible. If he suspected I was lying, he didn't let on. He turned to Krissy. "Stop by in the morning before you go to Lost Creek, and we'll figure something out."

CHAPTER TWENTY-FIVE

AS WE DROVE BACK to my place, I laid out my plan. "We'll go to Lost Creek tomorrow morning after we meet with the chief. It's easier to see what's coming at you in the daylight."

Krissy sucked in a breath. "Oh, God. I'm in danger, huh?"

I kept my voice even. "It's just best to be prepared. Meanwhile, how about the two of us doing a stakeout at your mother's tonight? Maybe we can catch whoever's harassing her. You game? If not, I'll do it myself."

She clapped her hands, almost giddy. "Ooh! A stakeout. Real detective stuff. Sounds like fun!"

I shrugged. "Not as much fun as you might think." I'd spent plenty of time in the recent past watching and waiting, hoping to catch some lowlife doing something they shouldn't be doing. Sitting in the car in the dark, my backside falling asleep, and my bladder begging for mercy. Definitely not fun.

Krissy said, "Much as I hate Fiona at the moment, she is *my* mother. And if you're willing to help *her*, then I should be willing to help *you*."

That's why, just after 10:00 p.m., Krissy and I were on Fiona's front porch, huddled under blankets in the dark and cold. We were both dressed totally in black, and I'd insisted we use camo makeup on our faces. "Otherwise, we glow in the dark."

We each had a thermos of coffee, and Krissy had slipped a couple shots of brandy in hers. She'd said, "Just the thing you need out in the cold." I didn't bother to tell her that alcohol only makes you *feel* warmer, making frostbite more likely. But we didn't have to worry about that tonight. The temperature hovered in the forties—cold enough but not below freezing.

An hour into the stakeout, my butt was numb. As I shifted from my left cheek to the right, I caught a shadow moving along the fence between Fiona's and Mrs. McGruder's yards. Someone in black, like us. A ski mask over their head. Carrying a sack of something.

I was sick of sacks. The sack of money. The sack of bones. What was in this one?

Krissy made a small noise. She'd spotted the figure too.

"Shh," I whispered. "Wait." I lowered my blanket and moved into a crouch position. Krissy did the same. We waited.

The figure crept closer. Tiptoeing across the lawn, glancing left and right. Then they disappeared from view.

A moment later, one of Mrs. McGruder's chickens let out a squawk, and the whole flock erupted. Her back porch light came on, and she burst from her back door—setting off the security flood lights in her yard, illuminating half the block. She screamed and swung a broom. "Get away from my chickens, you filthy beast."

In the lights, I saw a fat raccoon climb over the chicken coop fence and lumber off down the alley.

The hooded figure stood a moment in Fiona's side yard, taking in the ruckus in Mrs. McGruder's yard.

I jumped from the porch and ran, hunched low, ready to deliver a body slam.

At the last second, they saw me and swung the sack at my midsection. Something pointy jabbed me in the stomach and I folded over, hands pressed to my belly.

In the next second, gloved hands shoved me backward. My tailbone slammed into the packed earth. Pain shot up my spine.

The hooded figure watched me fall, then took off running down the alley.

I struggled to my feet, catching my breath as I staggered to the alley. They'd disappeared. Probably took off through a neighbor's yard. Impossible to know which yard, so it was futile to chase them. Besides, my backside hurt.

As I hobbled back to Fiona's house, I heard an engine start somewhere at the end of the block. Maybe it was the engine of a red truck. I had no way of knowing.

Mrs. McGruder had gone back inside her house. Krissy was waiting on Fiona's back steps, smoking a cigarette.

She said nothing about my hobbling. "Well, that was a big fat waste of time. I'm starving. Want to hit Burger Barn? They're open until two."

I scowled at her. "The last thing I need right now is a burger and fries. I'm exhausted and in pain. I need ice and my bed."

Krissy said, "Oh, well. I'm going to go inside and make a sandwich. I'll probably just crash here tonight."

So much for cousinly love and empathy. I said, "I thought you never wanted to see your mother again."

She stood and crushed the cigarette butt into the ground. "Yeah, I don't. But she *is* my mother after all. What can I say?"

"I get it," I said with a sigh. I turned to leave. "I'll pick you up in the morning around eight. We can go for breakfast before we meet with the chief."

"Let's make it later. My mom and I will probably be up late tonight, talking."

Of course, they'd make up after their big fight because, well, family is family.

CHAPTER TWENTY-SIX

WE GOT TO TRIMAK just after ten on Tuesday morning. The chief waved us into his office. He pointed at his laptop. "Just got the report from my buddy, the medical examiner. Have a seat."

I felt a familiar tension in my stomach. Hopeful, yet restrained. Not wanting to get too excited until I heard the facts. I took one chair, and Kris took the other.

The chief sat and looked at the computer screen. "The identification wasn't that complicated. The remains belong to a man named Clive Fenster. He was identified by his three gold fillings. He's been in the missing persons database for twenty years. You got lucky."

"Any other information?"

"Yes." He sounded excited. "Along with the bones, the bag contained some soil. 'Withee soil,' the report says."

"How is that helpful?"

"It narrows the burial site to within a few hundred miles."

"A few *hundred* miles? How is *that* helpful?"

He smiled. "It tells us this guy was buried within a few hundred miles of Three Rivers. Not Montana. Not Texas. Somewhere in our own backyard."

I would have figured that he was from the area, since his bones ended up in the area. But the chief seemed particularly jazzed about the soil thing, so I humored him. "So this kind of soil is special?"

"Not really. It's basically farm dirt. Good for hay. Common in areas with lots of dairy farms and alfalfa fields. Good for making hay to support the cows."

I frowned. "But Chief, you just described most of this state and the four states surrounding us. If the body was buried in a farm field, how do we figure out which one? It's the proverbial needle in a haystack."

He sat back in his chair and smiled. "I just think it's interesting how forensics can identify dirt like that. But it doesn't really matter because—and this is where we get *really* lucky—he was reported missing back then by his landlady." He paused for effect. "In Lost Creek."

I felt a shiver of excitement. Clive Fenster lived in Lost Creek. I looked at Krissy. "You ever hear of this guy?"

She shook her head.

I asked the chief, "Any speculation on how he died?"

He read the screen silently, then looked up. "If I'm correctly interpreting the medicalese in the report, it seems he died from a cracked skull. Maybe he took a hard fall."

My mind spun possibilities. "Okay, if he just fell and died, somebody would have buried him properly, right? But maybe someone whacked him and wanted to cover that up. Buried him in a farm field somewhere. Then, for some reason, dug him up and stuck him in that burlap bag. Then they put that in the old junker that Krissy drove here."

He gave me a bemused look. I interpreted that as admiration. He said, "Lots of possibilities, yes, but we don't know what actually happened, do we? We need to proceed with caution." He frowned at me. "Be careful, Mackenzie. We could have a murderer out there who doesn't want you digging things up, so to speak."

"Well, Chief, it seems things have already been dug up."

"Indeed, it does. And I know you. Be sure you wait for the cavalry before you go charging in. Promise?"

Again, that note of caution from the chief. I've come to accept his paternalistic caring for me. "I promise. I'll talk to the Lost Creek cops. See what they have to say."

"Sounds like a plan. Meanwhile, let's get your cousin fixed up."

I went to my office, and Krissy stayed with the chief. Twenty minutes later, she rapped on the door frame.

I looked up. "Whoa! I'd never recognize you!"

She was disguised as an old man. A very grungy old man. "Old man" is one of the chief's go-to undercover costume choices. I recognized the gray wig, the bushy eyebrows, and the thick black frame on the fake glasses.

She said, in a gravelly voice, "Hello there, Chickie. How do I look?"

I laughed. "The chief missed his calling. He should have been in the theater, in costume design."

IT WAS JUST BEFORE TWO IN the afternoon when we got to Lost Creek. We'd made good time, stopping only once on the drive, for gas station coffee and donuts, and for Krissy to buy cigarettes.

She chatted happily as we drove, excited about the "adventure" we were taking.

I finally said, "Krissy, Krissy, Krissy. You're heading back to people who are very angry with you. People demanding you return money you don't have. Counterfeiters. Mobsters."

I ignored the dirty look she gave me and continued, "And the bones? We don't know what happened to this Fenster guy. Could have been murdered. And who knows we have the bones? We don't know who we can trust. This isn't an adventure. We're heading into danger, and you need to take that seriously."

She crossed her arms and slumped back into the passenger seat, mumbling something about my taking all the fun out of it.

I let her sulk in silence for a mile or so, then said, "Kris, it's just that I have a bad feeling about all of this, and I don't like going into a situation where I have a bad feeling."

She rolled her eyes. "Quit worrying! Quit being such a dork, Dork! It's all gonna work out, you'll see."

It will all work out. Cockeyed optimist. That's Kris.

Lost Creek is about the most God-forsaken place in the state. It was a thriving fishing and resort community until time—and the interstate freeway system—passed it by. Now, it's a dozen blocks of deteriorating old buildings. Delport, an hour east, is where life thrives. Lost Creek got lost in the shuffle and just sits there, waiting for a tornado to wipe it out. If a town can feel sad, Lost Creek is it.

Krissy hunkered down in the passenger seat as we drove down the main street, not that anyone would have recognized her in that outfit. She pointed to a building of faded red brick with weather-grayed wood trim around grimy windows. The lower level still had a faded sign: JOHNSON MERCANTILE. Long out of business, from the look of the place.

"That's my apartment, up there." She pointed to the second story. "Right there, upper left corner."

I parked. We went up the exterior stairs on the side of the building to the apartment. Krissy unlocked the door, and we stepped into her old kitchen.

"Oh, my God," Kris whispered.

The place had been completely trashed. Dishes—cups, bowls, glasses—lay broken on the floor. A box of Oaty-Ohs and another box of Trix were emptied on top of the glass shards. The silverware drawer had been removed and dumped out. The freezer door hung open, and everything in it had thawed. Water dripped onto the floor.

In the living room, the couch cushions had been sliced open. The legs of a wooden end table had been broken off. A lamp was smashed, and its lampshade bore a dirty boot print.

"Somebody has been looking for the money, and they're not happy with you," I said. Snarky hissed. *Duh. Obviously. You're a genius, Sherlock.*

I followed Krissy into the bedroom. The mattress was slashed in several places. Why? If you hide money inside a mattress, you cut it open, and that spot would be obvious. Find that spot, find the money, right? The level of destruction in the apartment wasn't just somebody looking for something. This was fury.

She pointed at the dresser top. "Oh, no," she said. A jewelry box on the dresser lay in splinters. "My mother's jewelry is gone. I can't bring it back to her. Can't tell her I'm sorry for taking it." She looked away.

I put a hand on her forearm. "Maybe someday you can

buy something to replace it?" Snarky scoffed. *Again, Pollyanna? Stop being so sickeningly positive.*

Krissy evidently agreed with Snarky. She glared at me. "You just don't get it. It's not the same. I was in such a hurry to get out of here, I forgot the jewelry, and now it's gone. Forever." She sat on the edge of the shredded mattress, looking forlorn. "I'm just a screw-up. A loser. I mess things up all the time. Always have and always will!" With her elbows on her knees, and her face in her hands, she started to cry. Huge, racking sobs.

I sat beside her, my hand on her back. I tried to lighten the moment. "C'mon now. It's hard to see an old man cry."

She paused, then gave a little snort and wiped at her face with a sleeve. One of the bushy eyebrows was hanging down over her left eye. I pressed it back into place.

She said, "I really thought with all that money, I could finally get my life together."

I said, softly, "It's okay. We'll figure this out."

She sat another minute, then stood. "Let's get the hell out of here." She brought a black garbage bag from the kitchen, took the rest of the clothes from the closet and stuffed them inside. She picked through the debris scattered across the floor and added a few items to the bag.

She looked around one last time. "That's it," she said. "I don't give a shit about anything else here. Let's go."

Kris locked the door behind us. We drove away from the building, both of us scanning the street, looking for red trucks.

CHAPTER TWENTY-SEVEN

WE DROVE UP THE main drag—the only drag—in Lost Creek. "Stop here," Krissy said. She pointed at a little coffee shop called June's Place. "I want to say hello to my friend June."

I wanted to remind Kris that we weren't in town to make social calls, but a café owner in a small town often knows everything about everybody. *Gather information. Investigations 101.* I said, "Okay, but I don't want to leave Cricket out here on the street." Strange car in a small town. Too conspicuous.

Kris directed me to the parking behind the café. We went into the café through the back door. As we passed the kitchen, a large woman at the sink hollered over the running water, "Just take a seat, and I'll be right out."

Nobody else was in the café. Krissy whispered, "That's June back there," as we sat at a small table along the wall.

After a few minutes, June brought two brown plastic glasses of water to the table. Her pink tee shirt, stretched taut over her breasts and ample belly, said BLESS YOU! above a yellow daisy. "You're just in time. I was about ready to close up. Do you want menus?"

I said, "No. I'll just have one of those donuts." I pointed to the glass case on top of the counter.

She turned to Krissy. "And for you, sir?"

Krissy laughed. "June, it's me, Kris."

June squinted and got closer to Krissy's face. "Oh my gosh, Kris, I never would have recognized you."

I took that as a good sign. Krissy was safe in her disguise if even her good friend was fooled. June walked over to the door, locked it, and then flipped the sign hanging in the front window from OPEN to CLOSED. She pulled a chair from another table and sat with us. "What the heck are you doing back here? I heard Marcus was hot after you. Should you even be here?"

"Tell me what you've heard," Kris said.

June looked at me, then at Kris, and raised an eyebrow. Krissy said, "This is my cousin, Mackenzie. She's a detective. Show her your card, Mack." Krissy was obviously eager to impress her friend June with her amazing cousin, and I was happy to oblige. I handed June my TriMak card.

She read it out loud, then looked at me, eyes wide. "Wow. I've never met an investigator before. What kinds of things do you investigate?"

I sat back and crossed my arms, again the soul of modesty. "Oh, you know, the usual stuff you see on TV. Missing persons, stolen goods, cheating spouses." I didn't mention the missing parakeet I'd been asked to find. Or the mother who hired me to find her missing "boy," who turned out to be a thirty-something man shacking up with his girlfriend.

June shook her head. "Is it dangerous?"

I didn't want to recite the litany of dangerous, near-death moments I'd had, so I just shrugged. "Danger is just part of the job."

June looked at Krissy. "So you hired your cousin? What for?"

Krissy leaned toward her. "Two things. First, my mom is being harassed by somebody back in Three Rivers. Mack is going to figure that out. And second, I found a bag of bones." Kris paused for effect, then said, "They're human bones." Another pause. "As in a dead person."

June gasped and went pale. "Oh my God. Who is it?"

Before I could signal her to keep quiet, since I had no idea how the guy died or who might be involved—June could have been a murderer for all I knew—Krissy blurted, "A guy named Clive Fenster. Did you know him?"

June looked up at the ceiling, then at Kris. "Wow. I haven't heard that name in a hundred years. Sure, I knew him. Everybody knew him."

According to June, Clive Fenster arranged financing for local farmers when things were tough. "He was real creative that way. Clive got the money into the right hands, just in the nick of time—usually when the wolf was at the door." June told us that Clive Fenster was often able to help farmers facing foreclosure. But there were times when Clive couldn't pull a deal together. Despite his best efforts, people still lost their land or their livestock. "There are a few people around these parts who'd have nothing good to say about Clive Fenster."

"I'd like to talk with those people," I said.

June said, "You should go see Marietta French." June described a strong, resolute woman who'd inherited the family farm from her parents. The only child, she was determined to keep the farm going. "She hired help. Did her best. Never married. That farm was her whole life."

According to June, Miss French needed to raise some cash. Clive stepped in, worked his magic. "He arranged a loan for her with some money people out of state—Illinois, I think. When she couldn't make the payments, she forfeited her land to clear the debt." June shook her head. "All in the contract. All perfectly legal. Just not very nice."

My mind flashed back to the E-Z MONEY people. Also perfectly legal. Also not very nice.

June went on, "Marietta's farm was absorbed by a Big Ag company. They don't give a hoot about family farmers. Marietta was left with the house and less than an acre of a yard. Her father would have been so disappointed to see her lose it all. She was the fifth generation to farm that land. Such a shame. Just so sad."

June told me about another situation with a farmer named Lloyd Hollander. "Clive did the same kind of deal for him, and he lost his farm the same way. Lloyd lives with his daughter now over in Rock Falls. He'd be happy to hear Clive Fenster is dead, except he's got dementia. Probably doesn't remember what happened anymore. That's a mercy."

I hadn't thought about that before—that losing your happy memories also means forgetting the hard stuff too.

June said, "So do you have any theories about his death?"

I said, "Yes, we do. But I'm not going to speculate further until I investigate. And I'd appreciate you not saying anything to anybody about this."

June nodded and turned to Krissy. "So what's the deal with the casino, Kris? Folks are saying that Marcus was after you for cheating. That you and Jared Clark were in cahoots, and that the two of you ran off together. To Mexico, somebody said."

Krissy got indignant. "I won that money! I'm not a thief!" She crossed her arms and pouted, while I asked June what else she'd heard.

She looked at Krissy. "I heard that Delroy Bean traded cars with you."

Krissy's cheeks got red. "Delroy told people that? He swore he wouldn't tell anyone!"

June shook her head. "Honey, you never should have trusted Delroy. You know he ain't got the sense God gave him. And with you gone, he probably wanted to stay in good with Marcus." It was June's turn to lean in close. "You can tell me, Kris. Did you take the money? Did you rip Marcus off?" She leaned back. "Because, just so you know, if you did rip him off, nobody is going to tell the cops. Marcus is a crook, and everybody knows it. And you disappearing is the most exciting thing that's happened around here in ages. Taking the money from Marcus, well, that makes you like a female Robin Hood, taking from the rich. He's that evil guy in the story—what was his name?"

I said, "The Sheriff of Nottingham?"

"Yes! Marcus is him, and Kris is Robin Hood."

I looked at June. "How dangerous is this Marcus guy?"

"He wouldn't dirty his hands himself, but he has, um, connections, you know?"

"Are any of those connections named Slade? Or Jacko?"

"Yes, those two boys are buddies of his. They've always been trouble."

Possibilities lined up. Marcus sent Slade and Jacko to follow Krissy. They'd assumed the suitcase held all the money. They went back to Marcus—picture the Three Stooges, Moe slapping Curly—and he sent them back to Three Rivers for the rest.

They'd been following us around in that little red truck, trying to figure out where Kris had stashed the cash.

June continued. "Be careful with those two. They won't hesitate to hurt somebody."

"Thanks for the warning," I said. I'd had encounters with people who didn't hesitate to hurt others or just enjoyed seeing others suffer. Sick, twisted people. I thought about my aunt Fiona being harassed by someone. They hadn't made any overt threats, but that noose hanging in her plum tree sent a pretty clear message.

I tuned back in to the conversation as Krissy asked June, "So where is Marcus now? Do you know?"

"I heard Charlene say he went to Chicago. Something about casino business. You know Charlene comes here every day for lunch. If you come back tomorrow, you can catch her." June turned to me. "She's the assistant manager and the cashier over there, and she usually knows what Marcus is up to."

Kris and June obviously trusted Charlene, but I had my doubts. Grubb signed her paychecks. How trustworthy could she be?

I thanked June and got up. "Kris, we should probably get going if we're going to do what we came here to do before we head back to Three Rivers." I wanted to talk with Charlene Bean and try to talk with Jared again.

June stood, fluttering her hands. "Oh gosh, I never got you that donut."

"Don't bother," I said.

Kris pushed away from the table and gave June a hug. "It's nice to know there's another person in Lost Creek I can trust. You and Charlene have been good friends. Please don't say anything about seeing me here, okay? Not until Mack figures this whole thing out."

June patted her back. "You can trust me, sweetie."

As we came out of the alley behind June's, I spotted a red truck parked on the street by a U-Fill gas station. I slowed as I brought up the picture of the license plate on my phone. A match. "That's the truck we saw in Three Rivers."

She nodded. "Yep. It's got that white paint streak on the driver's side. Those two jerks are probably inside the gas station." She started to open the car door.

I grabbed her arm. "Whoa, Kris. Slow your roll. We need to run the plate, figure out who these people are before you go on the attack."

Kris slumped down in the seat and pouted, muttering something about already knowing who they were and something else about me not being the boss of her.

While she sulked, I called Heather Sullivan. Since she'd asked for my help with "snooping," I hoped she'd be in the mood to help me with ID'ing the plate.

Heather answered on the second ring and, without a hello, she asked, "You found something about the counterfeits?"

"No, sorry. It's something else. I need information on a red pickup with a white paint streak on the driver's side. Two guys have been following me." Okay, I fudged the truth there. I was actually the one doing the following in Three Rivers. "Can you run the plate for me?"

Heather said, "Has anyone threatened you?"

"No."

"Any reason to suspect there is criminal activity going on?"

"Uh, they stole my cousin's suitcase." I didn't mention the money that was in the suitcase. Illegal casino winnings and counterfeits. I didn't want to get into all of that.

A long silence from Heather, then she said, her tone flat,

"They stole a suitcase." More silence, then, "Did you witness that? Did you actually see them take the suitcase and drive away in this particular vehicle?"

"Well, no, but—"

She cut me off. "I have no reason to run the plate. Sounds like this vehicle has just been on the street at the same time you were. Not a crime, Prentice."

I grasped at a straw. "Maybe it's a stolen vehicle. You never know." That sounded lame, even to me.

"Nope. Not happening. Call me when you have something useful." She disconnected.

Snot. I made a face at my phone, then called the chief's cell. He picked up immediately. "What do you need, Chickie?"

"We're in Lost Creek, and I keep seeing the same red truck. I saw it in Three Rivers and now here. Detective Sullivan refuses to run the plate. You know a guy, right?"

"I know a lot of guys."

"You know a guy at the DMV?"

"If you want me to call in a favor, you need a good reason."

"Just a hunch, Chief. Isn't that reason enough?"

He went silent for a long moment. "You have a hunch."

"Yep."

Another hesitation, and then he said, "Text me the plate number."

I took that to mean the chief was starting to trust me a little, like maybe he thought I was becoming a detective who had good hunches or something. At least, that's what I was telling myself.

I felt proud.

CHAPTER TWENTY-EIGHT

KRIS WAS EAGER TO get to the casino to talk with her friend Charlene, but I suggested we first pay a visit to Jared Clark, the dealer.

Google directed us to a mobile home park a few miles outside of Lost Creek. BELLA VISTA consisted of a group of two dozen or so mobile homes. Driving past the first few homes, I concluded there was nothing "bella" or "vista" about the place. No beauty, no view.

One unpaved street led into the park. The first couple of homes were decent-looking, but they got progressively less decent as we drove. At the end of the drive, we found Jared's place, lot 23. A black metal two and a three were attached to the siding, but his name wasn't on the mailbox.

Half of a rusting bicycle was propped against the wall of a small shed in the side yard. Trash and beer cans were strewn across the lawn. Jared evidently enjoyed a party, and his friends weren't worried about littering.

The front door was ajar. I pushed it open. Krissy and I saw

Jared at the same time. He lay unconscious on the filthy carpet in the living room.

I ran to him and found a carotid pulse. "He's breathing. Barely. Call 911."

While Krissy reported the situation, Jared opened his eyes.

I said, "Jared, who did this to you?"

He had trouble talking through swollen, bloody lips. "Two. Never saw before."

Strangers. Maybe two of Grubb's friends from Chicago, looking for their money. Their fake money. I brought Jared a glass of water from his messy kitchen—a smaller version of the mess in his front yard. Krissy held his head up so he could take a gulp, then put a pillow from the couch under his head.

He squinted at her. "Old dude? Kris?"

"Yeah, it's me, Jared. In disguise."

I said, "You have to go to the hospital, Jared. You might have broken ribs." I looked at his hands, bruised and swollen, as if someone had stomped on them. "Or broken fingers." Hard to deal cards when your hands are smashed.

He shook his head. One eye had puffed shut, and he'd lost a couple of teeth. He slurred his speech, his tongue working as if he were trying to keep the rest of his teeth in his mouth. Through swollen lips, he said, "Two guys. Demanded money. Said I knew too much. Said they'd shut me up."

I felt a chill. "Jared, you're lucky they didn't kill you, stick you in the trunk of a car, and dump you someplace."

He mumbled, "Not lucky," and then groaned. "Neighbor. Yelled. They left."

"Your neighbor saved your life. Maybe your neighbor got a license plate number or can describe the guys. The local cops might be able to catch them."

Jared tried to laugh at that, but it came out as a little strangled sound.

Krissy snorted. "Yeah, that's not likely. The locals are probably buddies of theirs."

Jared moaned what sounded like agreement and tried to nod his head. The local cops were obviously looking the other way, allowing an illegal casino to operate in their backyard. Somebody was likely paying them off. How sad that a little town like Lost Creek would have so much corruption. You expect it in a big city. New York, Chicago, LA. Not in a little town in the middle of nowhere. *You're being naive, Sherlock.* Snarky was right.

I heard a siren in the distance, and soon red and blue lights flashed into the small living room. "They're here," I said.

"Crap," Jared said. He groaned again.

A brown-shirted Lakeland County sheriff's deputy stepped into Jared's living room, followed by two EMTs. Deputy Price took our statements. I told him about the neighbor, then gave him my card.

He said, "I'll call if I need anything more," with a tone that made it clear he was certain he wouldn't need me. For anything. Not ever.

As Krissy and I drove away, I said, "Obviously this is bigger than Lost Creek. Bigger than just an illegal casino. I'm worried about your safety. I don't want to take a chance that anyone else will recognize you. Do you think you can trust your friend June to keep her mouth shut about you being in town?"

"She's my friend."

"Trust her with your life?"

"Absolutely."

I suggested that Kris stay with June while I talked to the local cops.

She agreed, then said, "I just want to get my money. I won it fair and square."

I let out a sigh. "Like I said before, you can't keep money you won at an illegal casino. It's against the law."

"I don't care. Nobody has to know where it came from."

"But *I* know, Krissy, and *you* know. You say you didn't cheat but think about it. How well do you know Jared? What if he helped you win? You took the money. Marcus claims he wants the money back because you cheated, but he really wants it back because of the counterfeits that are in the mix. Jared tells you to run, figuring he'll track you down later and make you share the winnings by threatening to tell Marcus where you are. Still with me?"

"Yup."

"Meanwhile, your mother found the money and lost some at the casino. Now she'll be in trouble for spending money from an illegal operation. And Heather told us that fake twenties are showing up in Three Rivers at the Kwik Stop and the Tap. The trail of counterfeits leads right back to you, to your winnings. Jared's not in trouble for that, but you certainly would be."

Kris was quiet, then said softly, "This is one fine mess I've gotten myself into, isn't it?"

I said as I turned south, "This is one fine mess, indeed."

Kris asked, "So what do we do next?"

I said, "*We* don't do anything. *I* am going to talk to the local cops. *You* are going to stay out of sight, hopefully with your pal, June."

She started to protest, but I cut her off. "No, Kris, you stay with June. I'm going to the police station. You can't come along. In fact, don't talk to anyone while you're in town. We don't know who we can trust, and that includes the local cops. If you walk into the station, they might arrest you on the spot if they are in cahoots with Grubb. You need to stay with June for now. Agreed?"

She gave a huff, crossed her arms, and slouched in the passenger seat.

I chuckled. "It's funny to see an old man pout."

She stifled a snort.

The chief called as we pulled into the alley behind June's Place. On speaker, he said, "That truck came back registered to a Marietta French. Ring any bells?"

I took a beat, letting that register. "Definitely," I said. "You have an address?"

He said he'd text it. I thanked him and hung up, wondering how Marietta French was connected to Slade and Jacko, who were connected to Marcus Grubb, who was connected to some very, very bad people.

THE AIR INSIDE JUNE'S APARTMENT ABOVE the café smelled as good as Gram's kitchen on cinnamon roll day.

Kris, still a little pouty, asked June if she could wait there "while *Detective* Prentice takes care of some business." She emphasized the "detective" a little too much. I was getting tired of people's sarcasm.

June got excited. "Ooh, detective things! Yes, Kris, I'd love to have you stay. I just baked a batch of blueberry muffins, and I have beef barley soup on the stove."

She explained how to get to Marietta French's house. As

is so often the case, people in rural areas don't know actual addresses, just landmarks.

June said, "Take the main road out of town. Maybe four miles or so, you'll come to, uh, I think it's County Road B. You'll see a green barn with three gray silos. Turn right, then go about three miles. You'll see Marietta's place on the left, just past the church. You can't miss it."

She seemed sure of that. Me? Not so much. As I typed the directions into my phone, my stomach growled, partly because it always does when I get excited about a case. June heard my stomach making noises and insisted I take two blueberry muffins with me.

CHAPTER TWENTY-NINE

AS I DROVE AWAY from June's Café, munching a muffin, I heard the chief in my head. Always check in with the locals as a courtesy. Give them a heads up, just in case someone reports you as a suspicious stranger.

Housed in an old building off the main street, Lost Creek PD looked like a lot of other small-town stations I'd been in. A long counter separated the entry area from four desks, all vacant at the moment. The drab paint on the walls was scuffed and stained from who knows what.

I'd waited a few minutes when an older officer came from the back room. In his fifties, maybe, gray at the temples, but in good shape. The name tag on his dark blue shirt read ANDERSON. I presented my card.

He read it and asked, "What brings you to our little burg, uh, *Detective* Prentice?" *Another tinge of sarcasm? Seriously? I get no respect.* Officer Anderson had already ticked me off, and we hadn't even gotten started.

I said, "No need for the sarcasm."

He shrugged. "What do you need?" His tone implied that I should get to the point and quit wasting his precious time.

"I'm investigating the disappearance of Clive Fenster. You were here back then?"

He frowned, thinking. "Who?" Then the light dawned. "Oh, that guy. Yeah, I was here but that was, what? Twenty some years ago. Who cares about that now? Who hired you?"

"You know I can't tell you that."

He said, "All I can tell you is the guy left town and never came back. Case closed."

I could have told him about finding Fenster's bones, but I was feeling peevish. "Didn't it seem odd, him disappearing so completely?"

He shrugged again.

"You never followed up?"

Color rose to his cheeks as his jaw tightened. "Now you look here, young lady. We do our best to keep up with what we call crime around here. We don't have time to track down everybody who decides to leave town."

I held up my palms. "Okay, okay. Sorry. I didn't mean to imply that your department was negligent." I glanced around the place. "I'm sure you're very busy." I tried—honest, I did—but Snarky couldn't resist lobbing that little nugget of sarcasm.

He scowled. "My guess is you have *no* idea what we really do. Never spent any time wearing blue yourself. Just some twerp wannabe who decided it would be a lark to snoop around. Not sure what your deal is, but I got no time for amateurs."

Now he was just pissing me off. I pulled up to my full height, squared my shoulders. "Here's my deal. I am a licensed investigator. I was married to a cop. I work with the retired chief of Three Rivers PD. I've been around cops all my adult life. Not wearing the blue myself, true, but close enough to feel it, smell it, love it. I've put myself in harm's way plenty of times—almost burned to death, almost shot, nearly drowned, almost shoved off a cliff. Beaten up more times than I care to count."

I took a breath. My voice got louder. "I work hard to bring closure to people on cases that the cops don't have time for or have written off. When the cops got things wrong, I've tried to get them right. Things aren't always the way they appear, and that's what I investigate." I lowered my voice, leaned across the counter toward his face, parsing the syllables. "And I am *damned* good at what I do."

He leaned away, staring at me. Then he chuckled. "Well, I guess you told me what's what!" He extended a hand, and I shook it. "How can I help you, Detective Prentice?"

Respect in his voice. This was more like it.

He opened the swinging door next to the counter and waved me to the plastic chair by his desk. I accepted his offer of coffee. While he went to the Bunn coffee maker at the back of the squad room, I looked around.

His desk held a picture of a woman and two teenaged girls. An old computer monitor, at least ten years out of date, sat to the side. All along the edges, sticky notes of various colors held phone numbers and other information. One said PUSHUPS! Another had initials and dates—maybe reminders of birthdays.

He came back with two Styrofoam cups of coffee, handed me one and emptied the other into a white ceramic mug on his desk. HAPPY FATHER'S DAY it said, with a picture of a cartoon dragon on it. FROM YOUR LITTLE MONSTER.

"Cute cup," I said.

He smiled. "From my youngest." He pointed at the framed photo. "She's in college now. Her birthday is next week." He pointed at one of the sticky notes. "She'll be twenty-one. Hard to fathom."

"Time flies, huh?"

"Yeah, it sure does." He took a sip of coffee. His chair gave a squeak as he leaned back. "Now tell me why you're here."

I didn't want this guy to know that I knew an illegal casino was operating on his watch. If he knew about it, he was looking the other way, or worse, taking bribes.

"As I said, I'm investigating Clive Fenster's disappearance. I understand there were at least two people in the area who weren't fans of his."

"He did a lot of good for a lot of people around these parts. Helped to save farms and lent folks money when they needed it. Then he left town. Never came back." Anderson took a sip of coffee, then continued, "All efforts to track him were futile. Maybe he changed his name, his identity. No trace of him. Who knows what happened? He might have run his car off a cliff, into a ravine somewhere. Maybe he tried to go for help, but the wolves got him. No trace. Damnedest thing."

"What about the deals that didn't work out?" Was he going to tell me what I already knew?

"Yes, I recall there were a couple of deals toward the end that went south." He told me about Marietta French and Lloyd Hollander losing their farms.

"Any reason to think either of them would have hurt Fenster?"

"Hurt him? Nah. Miss French is the nicest person you'll ever meet."

"What about Hollander?"

He thought a moment, took another sip of coffee. "Some domestic calls out at the Hollander place back then. He took to drinking after he lost his land, started fighting with his wife. Can't blame the guy. A real family legacy like that—you don't want to be the guy who loses it. I can sympathize with the drinking. I recall the arguing got carried away on occasion, with a little bit of physical stuff, but nothing serious. And now he's got Alzheimer's. Living with his daughter. Harmless old guy."

"No thoughts that he might have become violent with Fenster?"

He shook his head. "Nah. In my experience, domestic stuff stays domestic, ninety-nine percent of the time."

And in Officer Anderson's opinion, domestic violence was evidently "nothing serious."

He gave me directions to the house where Lloyd Hollander lived with his daughter. He finished his coffee and stood. "If there's nothing else, I have to get out there. The mean streets of Lost Creek await." He chuckled.

I stood. "Just so I'm clear here, as far as you know, Clive Fenster made himself disappear. No foul play. Just"—I snapped my fingers—"pffft!"

"Yep. He's probably living high on the hog on some exotic island paradise."

I didn't say it. *Or he might have been murdered.* Officer Anderson would hear that Clive Fenster's bones had been found soon enough. I didn't want to tell him. I didn't want him to interfere with what I needed to do.

I needed more time to figure out what else was really going on with the casino, with the counterfeiting, and how it was all related, if it was, to Clive Fenster. And how his bones ended up in that burlap sack.

Anderson gave me his card with the same spiel I give others. "Call me if you think of anything . . ." blah, blah blah.

As I drove away, I thought about what he'd said—that domestic violence stays domestic, ninety-nine percent of the time. I asked Jimbo, "What about the other one percent, huh, Jimbo? If this Hollander could be violent toward those he loved, how much more violent could he be toward those he hated?"

Jimbo didn't answer, but I could tell he was thinking about it. So was I.

CHAPTER THIRTY

I FOUND MARIETTA FRENCH IN her front yard, spreading a layer of mulch over a flower bed to prep it for winter. The white frame farmhouse, with its sagging front porch, was badly in need of paint.

Miss French straightened up when she saw me drive up, then bent backward, hands on the small of her back, stretching. She was a sturdy-looking older woman, about my height, with long gray hair caught in a ponytail at the nape of her neck and a face creased from decades in the sun. I suspected there was a well-muscled torso under her faded denim shirt.

"Afternoon," she said.

I introduced myself and handed her my card.

Her eyebrows went up. "Investigations? You're a detective?"

"Yes, ma'am, I am."

She gave me a smile as she tucked my card into her shirt pocket. "What's this about?"

"Your red truck."

"I don't have a red truck."

"Your name is on the registration of a red truck involved in a crime in Three Rivers."

She got quiet. "Okay, I used to have a red truck, but my nephew bought it from me last year." She shook her head, disgusted. "Looks like he never bothered to change it into his name."

"Who is your nephew?"

Her eyes went icy. "I don't see how that's any concern of yours." Protecting the family. I'd have done the same thing, wanting to talk to my relative before I talked to anyone else.

Don't push. I switched topics. "I understand that you knew a man named Clive Fenster."

Her brows shot up. "I haven't heard that name in forever."

"You knew the man?"

"Yep, I knew that snake. Everybody around these parts knew him." A shadow crossed her face. "Thanks to him, I lost my land. Lots of people suffered because of him." She wiped her forehead with the back of her gloved hand and brushed a stray hair away from her face. "You want to know the worst part? Him showing off, like a fat cat in his fancy clothes, with that ruby ring and those gold chains around his rotten neck. Driving around in his fancy Cadillac. Showing off—we don't do that around here—knowing he got rich making other folks suffer. Like he was rubbin' our noses in it." She looked at the ground. "I imagine more than one person around these parts wanted to put an end to all of that." She met my eyes. "Nobody was sorry when he left town, the conniving rat. But that was a long time ago. Why you askin' now?"

I said in a measured tone, "It appears he never left town."

A subtle twitch in her left eyebrow. She said nothing.

People give you signals. I said, "He was killed and buried in this area."

Another slight twitch, and then a momentary direct look before she gave a snort of derision and turned away. "I don't know anything about that. Good riddance, if that's the truth. Now, if that's all, I've got chores to tend to." She resumed spreading her mulch.

Dismissed. "Please call me if you think of anything?"

She grumbled assent. She wasn't going to tell me anything more, so I left.

Sleet pelted Cricket's windshield as I followed the highway and then a county road toward—I hoped—Rock Falls and Lloyd Hollander. Twenty minutes later, I realized I had gotten lost.

GPS is reliable 99 percent of the time. I turned around, and after another twenty minutes of driving through increasingly heavy sleet, I knocked on the front door of the small frame house where Lloyd Hollander lived with his daughter.

A woman opened the door. A television blared from somewhere inside the house. I introduced myself and gave a generic reason for my visit. "Just need to talk to Mr. Hollander about something from long ago." I didn't mention Clive Fenster.

She told me her name—Adeline—and said, "My father is in the living room. He's going to take a nap as soon as *Judge Judy* is over, but you can speak to him if you wish. I have to warn you, he's not great at remembering things these days, but you're welcome to ask."

The old man sat in a recliner, eyes closed, chin resting on his chest. Judge Judy was reaming somebody out at full volume. Adeline turned the TV off, then shook her father's shoulder gently. She yelled, close to his right ear, "Dad? Someone is here to see you."

He opened rheumy eyes. I could tell he'd once been a big

man, a strong farmer. Big hands with the vestiges of old calluses rested atop the red knit afghan across his lap.

His daughter, standing behind me, said, in a low voice, "He doesn't hear very well. You'll have to yell."

I said, loudly, "Mr. Hollander, I'm Mackenzie Prentice. I have a few questions for you, sir."

He looked up, confusion on his weathered face. It took a moment for him to focus on me. "Uh huh," he said with a slight nod.

"I need to ask you about Clive Fenster."

He sucked in air and his face went dark. He shouted, "Liar! Cheat!"

I shouted back. "What was the problem?"

"Damn him!" He shook a fist in the air. "Liar! Cheat!"

I dodged the fist that swept perilously close to my face.

His daughter stepped in front of me, took her father's hand, and patted it back onto his lap. "It's okay, Dad. It's okay." She spoke softly, her touch communicating comfort to the old man. He sank back in the recliner, let out a sigh, then closed his eyes.

The daughter turned to me. "I'm sorry. I'm afraid he won't be able to help you today. He needs to rest now."

As she ushered me into the hallway, I asked, "Would you be able to tell me about his troubles with Mr. Fenster?"

She hesitated and then said, "I only heard about it after the fact. After Dad lost the farm. I was living in Minneapolis at the time. I came back home after I retired to help my parents. Mom passed eight years ago, and Dad's been with me since then. I know he blamed Fenster for having to sell the farm, but I don't know the details. My parents never wanted me to worry about them. They kept their troubles to themselves. Why do you ask?"

"We believe Mr. Fenster may have been killed."

She sucked in her breath. "And you think my father had something to do with that? Ridiculous!"

"He seems pretty angry at the guy, even after all this time," I said.

"It's the dementia. He's never gotten angry enough to hurt anyone before!" She looked at the floor, hesitated, then cleared her throat. "Okay, so he punched a cow once. And once in a while, he kicked one of the dogs away from the cows. But to actually hurt another person? Never." She met my eyes and shook her head. "No, he'd never be capable of doing anything like that. Now if you'll excuse us . . ." She led me to the front door and opened it.

I handed her my card. "If you think of anything else—"

She accepted the card but shook her head. "There's nothing else. My father could never have hurt anyone. That's that." She seemed so certain, I hoped it was true, for her sake and for her father's.

She said goodbye and closed the door behind me, rather more firmly than was necessary.

CHAPTER THIRTY-ONE

IT WAS EASIER NAVIGATING away from Rock Falls than it was getting there. As I drove, I thought about my conversations with Lloyd Hollander and Marietta French.

Thanks to Clive Fenster, they both ended up losing everything. Fenster must have been a slick salesman, a smooth talker who was able to speak the farmers' language. Since the local farmers trusted him, he was likely trustworthy at first. He arranged financing for folks, and they appreciated it.

Then something changed. But what? The source of the financial help? Some connection with someone with connections to what June had called "Big Ag," whatever that meant. I'd heard about corporate farming, with big enterprises buying up smaller, family operations. Often when the family farmers were under financial duress.

I could imagine a farmer selling land to a corporation like that—taking advantage of that opportunity—if he was ready to retire or had other reasons to sell. But that would be a choice the farmer made, not something forced on him because someone got fancy with the financing, jacked up the interest rate, and then, when he couldn't make the payments, pushed him into a sale.

I felt a hot pulse of anger. That kind of situation was similar to Fiona getting into trouble with the E-Z MONEY people. Hers on a much, much smaller scale, of course, but the effect was the same. Misery.

So people were upset with Fenster. Understandably so.

Did Lloyd Hollander crack Fenster in the skull with a shovel? Or did Marietta French push him from the second story hay loft of her barn?

Ooh, ooh! Real life game of Clue! Rational Me loves that.

I assumed that whoever killed him buried him in a farm field somewhere in the vicinity, but there were thousands of acres of "Withee soil" in this area.

Needle, meet haystack.

We start with what we know. Somebody dug up Clive Fenster, put his bones in a burlap sack, and stuck that in the trunk of a junker at Delroy Bean's garage.

Delroy Bean. Start there.

I followed the GPS directions, hoping they'd be correct this time, toward Bean's Repair and Restoration. Ten miles outside of Lost Creek in the opposite direction from Rock Falls.

The sleet had turned to snow. Large flakes drifted down, melting as they hit the hot metal of Cricket's hood, and whitening the farm fields on either side of the road. After several curving miles, GPS informed me that my destination was on the right.

Sure enough.

Delroy Bean's business was marked by a huge home-made-looking metal sign, rusting and hanging slightly crooked from a wooden frame next to a rutted dirt driveway.

BEANS

He'd missed the apostrophe.

REPAIR & RESTORATION

From the look of the place, neither of those happened very often. A veritable graveyard of old cars, an acre of rusting metal, skeletonized for parts, lay beyond the small building marked OFFICE.

I peered through the grimy door glass of the office. A man in grubby coveralls was hunched over a keyboard, squinting at the monitor. His fingernails were thick with grease, as you'd expect from someone in his line of work. But the greasy look extended up the sides of his neck, across his face, and into the dirty brown hair slicked back from his forehead.

Snarky couldn't resist. *Who needs hair gel when you've got 10W-40?*

I rapped on the glass. He looked up, closed the computer quickly, and waved me in.

"Delroy Bean?"

"That's me," he said, his tone jovial. One of his brown eyes drifted to the side as he looked at me. I judged him to be in his late forties and maybe five foot nine. He was missing one tooth—his upper front left incisor. Nothing wrong with Delroy Bean that a good dentist, and a good eye surgeon, couldn't fix.

He gave me a gap-toothed grin. "What can I do ya for?"

I handed him my card as I introduced myself.

He went pale, stumbled back, and plopped into the desk chair. "I didn't know she was married! She told me she was separated. I swear!"

Interesting. Delroy had a girlfriend. A married girlfriend. Advantage, Mack. Play this out. "Well, she *is* married, Mr. Bean, and you'd better stop what you're doing immediately. Obey the order to cease and desist, or you'll end up in jail!" *Liar, liar, pants on fire!*

He nodded quickly and held up both hands. "I get it! No need for the law to get involved."

I pressed my advantage further. "I'm here about *another* matter as well, Mr. Bean. It's come to our attention that you concealed a corpse."

He stood. "Now hold on just a second there. I never did do no such thing! I got no idea what you're talking about!"

I read sincerity in his tone and on his face, from which all color had drained.

I waved a hand toward the junkyard. "A body was discovered in one of your vehicles. What do you know about that?"

He scowled, his face reddening under the grease. "I don't know what in hellfire yer talkin' about! I admit to messin' around with Jessie, but you tell her husband that's all done now. And I don't know nothin' about no dead bodies. You stop harassin' me and get outta here right now, or I'll call the sheriff!"

I'd come to the end of my advantage, and I didn't want him to get mad enough to call the local cops on me. "Fine, Mr. Bean. I'll leave." Then I couldn't help but add, "Expect to hear from the others soon."

Sometimes I just make stuff up like that. Not nice, I know. I turned and walked out as he begged for clarification.

He yelled, "Hey, you wait a minute! What others? Who you talkin' about?"

I waved a hand. Dismissed.

As I started Cricket, he yelled from the office doorway. "What others? WHAT OTHERS?"

I drove away, watching in the rearview as he shook a fist at me and then gave me the finger. I'd upset Delroy Bean, and I was curious to see what he'd do about it.

The snow was coming thicker now. Dense sheets of wet flakes were quickly piling up on the ground beside the road. I ran my wipers to clear the windshield. At a stop sign, I checked the weather app on my cell. The map showed this was the leading edge of a huge mass of snow on the way. This happens sometimes in late autumn. The surprise snowstorm.

It was after three as I drove back toward Lost Creek. It would be dark by four-thirty. Days are short this time of year. I'd planned to pick Kris up from June's and then go to the casino to talk with her friend Charlene.

But given the weather, it was probably wiser to pick her up and head back to Three Rivers. This is how we function in the north country. Everything is "weather permitting," and plans can change abruptly.

I had the wipers on high, and they were having trouble keeping up with the thick, wet snow, which was now starting to accumulate on the surface of the highway. I took a curve a little too fast and felt the beginnings of a fishtail in the car's back end. I took a deep breath to calm my racing heart, slowed down, and turned on the front vent to keep the windshield from fogging up.

I passed a group of several large warehouses with a big sign: LONGACRE FEED AND SEED. The yard was full of semi-trucks. Railroad tracks ran behind the complex.

As I approached the railroad crossing, the bells started and the crossbuck lights flashed, as the red-and-white striped safety barriers dropped into place. Cricket's tires skidded a little as I braked, stopping inches from the gates. I heard the blast of a train horn to my right, where the tracks curved behind a big hill. I could hear the horn but couldn't see the train.

I leaned back in the driver's seat and talked to Jimbo. "This is so typical. Just my luck. The train always comes when I'm in a hurry. Or the place closes five minutes before I get there. Or the suspect leaves right before I arrive. 'You just missed him. If you'd only gotten here a minute earlier.' Just how it goes for me, Jimbo . . . story of my life."

I thought maybe I could find another road, where the train had already crossed, to get back to June's. Just before I could put Cricket in reverse, intending to back up and turn around, a black pickup truck with a snowplow attached to the front came up behind me and bumped into my car.

"Whoa!" I yelled. Obviously, the driver wasn't paying attention, going too fast for the slippery conditions. In my rearview mirror, I couldn't make out the driver's face. He had a black baseball cap pulled low over his eyes. At least, I thought he was a he.

I had my hand on the door handle, ready to get out and check the damage, when I noticed in my side mirror that the truck had backed up. *Nice, since I want to back up too.* I shifted into reverse, but before I could move, the black truck roared forward and slammed into my car again.

This time hard. Very hard.

Cricket flew forward and smashed through the gates. My head jerked backward and hit the headrest. Then my face smacked into the steering wheel.

I felt a sharp pain up the side of my neck, and everything got fuzzy.

CHAPTER THIRTY-TWO

A SECOND LATER, LOUD CHIRPING snapped me back. Jimbo was going nuts. "Chirrup! Chirrup! Chirrup!"

I immediately felt vibrations coming up through the floor of the car.

I opened my eyes. The safety gates, designed to break away in such a circumstance, lay in pieces on the ground around my car.

The car was on the tracks. *I* was on the tracks.

The train was coming fast.

I turned the key. *Click click.* Nothing. The ramming from behind and the impact with the crossing barrier had killed the engine.

"CHIRRUP! CHIRRUP! CHIRRRRRRUP!"

"I'm trying, Jimbo!" I fought tears. "Come on! Come on!" I begged the car to start.

I did what I imagine everyone does in a moment like that—I kept doing the thing that wasn't working, expecting different results. Insanity.

The train blasted a warning as it closed in on us. Its brakes screamed, metal on metal. *Skreeeeeeee!*

I knew—I just knew, you know?—that train wasn't going to stop. It would hit my car. I would die.

I should have jumped out and run for cover. I didn't. I had a crazy thought of not wanting to leave Jimbo. Again, insanity.

I squeezed my eyes shut, begging the universe or whoever might be listening, and gave the key one last crank.

Cricket sprang to life. I shifted, floored the accelerator, and the car jumped forward. A second later, the whole frame shuddered violently as the train roared past, inches behind us.

Heart hammering, shaking head to toe, I pulled to the side of the road and shifted into park. I folded my arms across the top of the steering wheel, lowered my head onto them, and sobbed. And sobbed. Relief. Anger. Then relief again.

I heard a rap on the window. A woman stood outside—early fifties maybe—concern etched on her face. Her car was parked on the opposite side of the road.

I lowered the window.

She said, "Oh my God. I saw what happened. Are you all right?"

I assured the stranger, "I'm okay, I'm okay." I stared a moment at her hair—snowflakes were landing, so softly, on her head. *Look at the tiny snowflakes, tiny snowflakes, tiny snowflakes. Are you an angel?*

I felt the urge to laugh. I kept staring as the snowflakes drifted down. I wanted to reach out and catch one.

She furrowed her brow. "You don't look okay. You're bleeding."

I checked my face in the visor mirror. A trickle of blood traced down my right cheek from a small cut on my forehead.

My lower lip felt fat, and I'd bitten my tongue. I touched the cut, then my lip. "All thuper . . ." I searched for the rest of the word. "Superficial, thath's it. All thuperficial." I was lisping a little.

"Do you want me to call for help?" She had her cell in her hand.

I shook my head to clear it. "No, really, I'm okay. I just need a minute."

"Okay, but I really think you should get checked out."

"I will, I promith. Right now, I need to get back to town." *Three Rivers? Lost Creek? Where am I going?*

She said, "That was really close. I thought for sure the train was going to hit your car. I'm so glad you're okay. You sure you are?"

"Did you see the black truck?"

"What truck? I only saw your car on the tracks as I pulled up."

Whoever had done this to me would remain a mystery for the moment. But there couldn't be that many black pickups with snowplows around, could there?

I nodded, thanked her and put Cricket into drive, and rolled on toward Lost Creek. She did a U-turn, pulled in behind me, followed me for half a mile, then gave a quick honk and a wave as she turned down a side road.

My thoughts cleared as I drove. *Lost Creek. Get Krissy.*

Back at June's, I took photos of Cricket's damage. The front grill was dented from crashing through the railroad crossing gates. The back end fared worse from the impact with the black truck's plow blade. One taillight was smashed, the back bumper was bent inward, and the back liftgate refused to open. I'd need to get repairs done back at Dan Webster's garage in Three Rivers. I certainly couldn't go to Bean's.

I knew I needed to report the damage at the railroad crossing, but who could I trust? Officer Anderson? Anxious Me got a little nervous. *Can we really trust him? He could have been driving the pickup, for all we know.* I pushed that thought away. The railroad crossing was likely in Lakeland County territory. I looked online for the non-emergency number for the sheriff's department and left a voicemail with the details. Before I disconnected, I suggested they talk with Delroy Bean, since I knew he wasn't happy with me. *There you go, Mr. Bean. The "others" want to talk to you.*

I disconnected and went upstairs to retrieve Krissy. She took a look at me and freaked out. "Oh my God! You're bleeding!"

June went into nurse mode, wet a cloth and cleaned my forehead, then put two Band-Aids across the cut. "Don't worry. It's superficial," she said, not lisping at all.

My head hurt. I explained what happened. "June, do you know who drives a black truck with a plow? I couldn't get a plate, and I think the driver was male, but I can't be sure."

June said, "Everybody and their uncle has a truck with a plow around here this time of year." She squinted at my face. "You shouldn't be driving. You might have a concussion. I'd offer to let you both stay here, but as you can see, I don't exactly have room for guests." The apartment above the café was just one big room, half of it the kitchen, with a bathroom at the far end. June didn't even have a couch, just a recliner aimed at the TV.

Krissy said, "That's okay. We'll get a room at the Sundowner Motel." She looked at me. "It's just down the road, and I'm driving. Don't argue."

Kris thanked June for her hospitality. June insisted we take a care package to the motel with us. Into a brown grocery bag, she set a bag of six muffins, a bottle of orange juice, two roast beef sandwiches, and a bag of potato chips. She added two huge chunks of chocolate cake with thick chocolate frosting wrapped in tin foil, plastic utensils, and two Styrofoam cups. "That should hold you for the night," she said. She hugged us both, and we left.

The snowstorm was winding down. A county truck had cleared the highway. I thought about the truck that had hit me. The intent was obvious: to have the train hit my car. To have me dead. Who wanted that so badly?

The last light flakes of snow continued to fall as Krissy drove to the Sundowner. I explained that I had a small suitcase—a.k.a. BOB—in the back of the car. "BOB is short for bug-out-bag, and he's in my car all year long, especially in the winter. My mom says you never know when you might run into bad weather and need to hole up in a motel." Bob has everything—toiletries, snacks, medicines—anything you could possibly need in an emergency.

"Your mom cared about you kids," Kris said. "She still does. You're lucky."

"Your mom cared about you, too, Krissy."

"Ha! Nice that *you* think so. After my dad died, I could have disappeared, and she wouldn't have even noticed. Here's an example. Senior year, I went to the prom with that guy—you remember Drake?"

"He went to prison later, didn't he?"

"Yeah, in his twenties. But on prom night, he didn't even pick me up. I had to get a ride to the dance with my friend Jill and her boyfriend. My mother had never even met Drake. For all she knew, I was going to the dance with an axe murderer. You know what she said to me when I left?"

She waited for an answer from me. My head was throbbing, so all I could muster was a half-coherent, "Wha--?"

"She asked me if I was gonna be home for breakfast. That's it. Not 'Who is this guy?' or even 'Hope you have a good time.' Nothing! Just was I going to be home for breakfast."

I mumbled, "That sucks."

"Yeah, my life sucked. Seriously. She didn't give a flyin' fig about me. Didn't then and doesn't now. If she cared, she wouldn't have taken my money. She'd have a place for me to sleep. She'd clean up all that crap in her house and not just leave it for me to clean up after she's dead. And she would have quit drinking years ago."

I felt sad, as I had before, imagining Krissy growing up in Fiona's house.

We checked in at the Sundowner office, then Krissy parked Cricket in front of room 15. This is the kind of motel where you park right in front of your room. We went inside, Krissy towing BOB. Then she fetched ice from the machine by the motel office.

I took four extra-strength Tylenols, then wrapped some ice cubes in the free shower cap from the motel bathroom. I alternated holding the ice against my lip, then pressing it against the cut on my forehead, while I tried to focus on whatever Krissy was watching on TV.

She was still in the old man clothes, sans wig, glasses, and eyebrows. We hadn't planned to spend the night in Lost Creek. I had extra clothes in BOB, but none that would fit Kris. She had some other clothes from the apartment but left them out in the car. She said she felt safer in the disguise. Personally, I wouldn't have slept in the grubby old man clothes, but to each her own.

By the time the ice melted, the Tylenol had dulled the ache in my neck and the pain in my head. I fell asleep, leaving Krissy in the next bed, eating everything in the bag from June's and laughing at Jimmy Fallon's antics on *The Tonight Show*.

CHAPTER THIRTY-THREE

I WOKE THE NEXT MORNING just before seven, surprised that my head felt okay. No headache. A slight stiff neck was the only reminder that the attack at the railroad crossing wasn't just a bad dream. Someone didn't like me very much. Didn't like me snooping around. Someone wanted me to go away. Maybe permanently.

I rolled over and looked toward Krissy's bed. The bed was empty, the covers rumpled. The bathroom fan was running. I lay in bed as long as I could. At that point, nature wasn't just calling—it was screaming my name.

I rapped on the bathroom door. "Kris? I need the bathroom."

No answer. I knocked again, louder, then opened the door.

No Kris. Next to the sink lay the bushy eyebrows, wig, and black-framed glasses the chief had given her. As if she'd melted and left those things behind. *Silly thought.*

I quickly took care of business, and then, since there were no other spaces Kris could be *inside* the room, I checked outside.

The snow had stopped sometime during the night. There

was an inch or so on Cricket's roof, and on the three other cars in the lot. I looked left and right. No sign of Krissy.

I shivered in the morning chill, then went back inside to think. Maybe she'd walked down to the motel office for some reason.

I dressed quickly in jeans and TriMak sweatshirt, socks, and Doc Martens. I grabbed the key card, closed the door behind me, and trotted down the narrow sidewalk to the right, toward the motel office.

A very skinny woman, fifty-ish, with ridiculous magenta hair and gigantic gold hoop earrings, was perched on a stool, watching *Good Morning America* on a tiny television set at the end of the counter.

"Have you seen my cousin? She was here last night." I described Krissy. "Tall woman, white hair cut short, streaks of color in it? Kind of loud?" I didn't say, *And kind of crazy*. "You can't miss her."

She shook her head. "Nobody's been around this morning but me."

As I walked back to the room, I noticed a cigarette butt on the sidewalk in front of our room. I picked it up. Could've been a Camel, Krissy's brand, given the mottled paper on the filter.

A theory formed. She got up sometime during the night and stepped out front for a smoke. I stood outside the room door, imagining the scene. *Must have been cold out here. She stood here smoking, watching the snow fall.*

I said aloud, "Then what, Krissy?" Had Krissy come out to retrieve something from Cricket? I looked down at the pavement around my car. No footprints. I glanced at the car a couple doors down to the right, in the direction of the office. No footprints in the snow.

To the left, I noticed one long mark in the snow of the parking lot. My stomach knotted as my throat tightened. I stepped forward.

A drag mark. I crouched to get a closer look. Definitely a drag mark. Not like suitcase wheels being dragged through the snow. More like human feet being dragged.

My imagination kicked into high gear. Marks of a scuffle in the snow. Krissy fighting back.

More drag marks. Krissy overpowered.

I stood up. Krissy dragged to a vehicle, whose tire tracks in the snow then led across the parking lot and out.

I racked my brain. *Had I heard a yell in my sleep? Had she cried out for help?* I'd been sleeping so soundly. Maybe she'd yelled, but I didn't hear. The knot in my stomach got tighter with the shame of having failed to protect my cousin.

Stupid, stupid, stupid! Snarky can be relentless.

I needed to find Kris. I threw our stuff together, tossed BOB into Cricket, and drove to the motel office. I left the car running, ran inside, signed the receipt, and shoved my TriMak card at the magenta-haired clerk. She promised—with an enthusiastic nod that sent her giant hoops swinging—to call if she heard anything.

I drove away from the Sundowner. Krissy had been taken, of that I was certain. And I was sure who'd taken her. Marcus Grubb. Maybe not him personally, but his henchmen.

Rational Me weighed in. *Henchmen? Minions? He's not exactly an evil genius.*

Badass took charge. *The guy is slime, and he's got Krissy. Let's go get her!*

I'd driven fifteen minutes toward the casino when the motel clerk called. "Just wanted to let you know that another guest heard someone arguing in the middle of the night. She said she peeked out the window and saw two men and a woman getting into a truck. Could that have been your cousin?"

Maybe, or maybe just someone stopping at the motel for a quickie. "Any description of the truck, or the people?"

The clerk said, "She didn't get that good a look. Didn't want to be involved. She wouldn't have said anything, except I asked her when she checked out." She assured me she would ask everyone else at the motel and call me with any information. "This is so exciting. Nothing like this has ever happened to me before!"

"Happened to *you*?"

She gave a breathless giggle. "I just mean I've never been part of an investigation before. It's exciting." She paused. "Oh, I don't mean it's exciting—or good—that your cousin is missing. But, oh, you know what I mean."

"I do." Civilians often get a thrill when they get close to my line of work. I understand that because I used to feel the same way. But after you see enough of the dark side of human nature, it all starts to wear a bit thin.

I thanked her and ended the call.

Drive time is always good thinking time. Krissy was grabbed, probably by Marcus Grubb's guys. I wasn't sure what all Grubb was doing, besides running the illegal casino, but it had something to do with funny money. And maybe Clive Fenster's bones.

My Spidey senses tingled. I was getting close. Closer and closer. Badass Me outlined my next steps:

Find Kris.

Find evidence to send Marcus to prison.

Get home for Thanksgiving.

Easy peasy, lemon squeezy.

CHAPTER THIRTY-FOUR

THE SNOW HAD BEEN cleared from the highway to the casino, piling up in mounds along the edges of the road. Stubbles of cornstalks poked through the snow in the fields. The storm had passed, but the low, gray ceiling of sky remained sullenly clouded. Hills and valleys rolled by, but I paid little attention. I had one focus: Find Krissy. Fast.

Anxious Me was afraid I'd be too late, that whoever had taken her would hurt her. Anxious worried that they'd hurt me too.

At the same time, Badass Me was ready to charge in full force and save the day.

Rational Me echoed the chief's advice: *Don't go in without backup.* But under these circumstances, who would that be?

I didn't know who I could trust in Lost Creek. Officer Anderson seemed a decent sort, but the illegal casino had been operating under his nose for years. June from the café? No help there if things got dicey.

My backups were in Three Rivers, and it would take time I

didn't have for someone to get to Lost Creek. I called the chief, got his voicemail, and explained what was going on. Just knowing he knew the situation gave me comfort.

Trip and Sheena were skiing somewhere in Colorado. And Germany, untrained, would likely be more hindrance than help.

Vince came to mind. He and Krissy had a thing going. He'd be willing to help me find her, but I didn't want to see his stupid face. Nick? Nope. He was a lost cause.

Marcus Grubb obviously had connections with some very bad people—just ask Jared Clark—and I didn't know what I'd be getting into. I needed heavy-duty backup, and I had only one option left.

I called Heather Sullivan.

She picked up immediately. "You got something?"

"Not anything on the funny money. At least, I don't think so. But I need your help."

She couldn't hide her disappointment. She let out a sigh. "I already told you I'm not running that plate." I sensed the eyeroll behind her words.

I said, "It's not about that. My cousin Krissy is missing. Somebody grabbed her. I think it's connected to this illegal casino outside of Lost Creek. I'm on my way to find her, and I could use some backup." I reminded her how I'd come to the rescue when a sleazebag she'd met online attacked her in Donatello's parking lot.

She paused. "Nobody else available?"

I filled her in on the chief and Trip's whereabouts.

She sighed. "It's way out of my jurisdiction. What about the locals?"

"Not sure I can trust them. This casino has been going for years. The local cops might be dirty, taking bribes."

She gave a low growl. "I hate dirty cops."

As enticement, I added, "And the fake money might be coming from this casino, and there might even be involvement from the Chicago mob."

She paused, then said, "That makes it a federal case. I don't need to be stepping on any toes. I'm going for a promotion, and I need to go by the book."

I reminded her that she'd asked me to snoop into the counterfeit money floating around Three Rivers. "So you involving me in that investigation was by the book? What would your boss think about that?"

Bordering on blackmail? Snarky was impressed.

"Well . . ." She paused for several moments, then let out a sigh and said, "Fine. I'll help you. But then we're even, okay?"

I told her how to find the casino and said, "I'm heading there now."

"Wait for me. An hour and a half, max, provided the highways are clear. Just wait for me."

"Krissy doesn't have time for me to wait." I disconnected and drove on toward the casino.

CHAPTER THIRTY-FIVE

THE BARN LOOKED LIKE a thousand other barns from the outside. You don't exactly put up flashing neon lights when you're operating illegally. Only the double row of cars parked outside offered any indication that the place wasn't full of cows.

I parked Cricket at the end of the second row of cars. I checked the time. Eleven in the morning, and the place was busy. I looked around to be sure I was alone in the lot, then hurried toward the casino, staying close to the outside wall.

I crept up to the door and peeked inside. The barn had been remodeled, a hardwood floor added. I'd seen enough casino interiors on TV to guess what I was looking at. Several tall tables for roulette or craps. Shorter tables—a half dozen or so—might be for poker games. Slot machines lined the far wall, where people hunched, mesmerized by the rolling images. Hoping dreams would come true with the next pull of a lever.

No windows. No clocks. No sense of time or season. Just the cacophony of bells, clicks, buzzes, and rattles, and the lights—flashing excitement red, promising yellow, come-hither gold. Another world. A fantasy world tucked inside an old barn in the middle of Nowhere, USA.

A young woman at a table dealt blackjack to three customers. Maybe she'd taken Jared's place, since he was out of commission. I hoped he'd be okay. Whoever beat him up had done a bang-up job, and he was lucky to be alive. I cringed, remembering how they'd stomped and crushed his hands. Such cruelty. Poor Jared. His poor hands.

At the far end of the barn, the cashier's booth stood next to an unmarked door that likely led to the office. A guy in black, with massive muscles, stood on alert near the door. Buzz cut, black shirt, rippling pecs, and thick biceps. Security, no doubt. They always look like that. Military-trained maybe. Maybe a member of the Chicago crew.

No sign of Slade or Jacko. I decided that if Krissy were on the premises, she wouldn't be in the casino. Too many people around.

I turned to go back outside when the office door opened. A woman with long gray hair hanging loose emerged, carrying a duffel bag. Marietta French. She said something to Mr. Security. He laughed, and she went out the side door of the barn.

I stepped outside and stood close to the building, waiting. A minute later, a vehicle came around the corner from the far side of the casino.

A black pickup truck with a plow on the front.

And Marietta French at the wheel.

She'd rammed my car onto the tracks. She wanted me to die. Why? I tried to recall the conversation we'd had in her yard. She'd told me she'd given her red truck to her nephew. She'd refused to name him. Was it Slade? Jacko? Mr. Security? Marcus? Or somebody else?

As far as Marietta French knew, I was just investigating Clive Fenster's death. What was her connection with all of this? Why did she want to silence me?

I wanted to follow her and demand answers, but those answers would have to wait. Right now, I had to find Krissy.

I went back to the car to get my TriMak flashlight, the police-grade, heavy-duty piece of equipment the chief calls "the great persuader." I was operating on my hunch that Grubb had Krissy somewhere close to his lair. What if I was wrong about that? She could be anywhere in thousands of acres of farm fields and forests. Abandoned properties. Construction sites. Anywhere.

Badass weighed in. *Quit doubting yourself. Start with what you know.*

What I knew: Marcus Grubb was in the middle of all of this, funneling funny money through his casino, probably for the Chicago syndicate.

Anxious Me shuddered. *Gangsters. Sleeping with the fishes. Making offers you can't refuse.*

Rational Me said, *Calm down. This isn't some old-timey gangster movie. Stick with the facts.*

The facts: There are other buildings on this property. Search for Krissy here first.

I hugged a line of pine trees on the west side of the field. I looked around to be sure nobody else was out here. Everybody else was enjoying the ambience of the casino. Nobody cared about a random woman snooping around old farm buildings.

I left the shelter of the pines and trotted toward a long, low building that had peeling red paint and faded green trim. No sign of footprints anywhere near it. I moved to the next structure, a few yards away. It reminded me of the corn crib on my grandparents' farm. I saw tracks. Deer tracks. Bambi passing through. The extended footprints of a rabbit bounding by.

I pulled on the door. It hung loose on one hinge. I swept the space with the light beam. Old farm implements, rusting in piles. No sign of recent activity of the human kind, just the sound of about a million mice scurrying out of sight. I shivered. I'd had enough contact with field mice to last my lifetime.

A sudden gust of icy wind whipped across the field and straight through me. I reached inside my jacket, pulled the hood of my TriMak sweatshirt up over my head, and tightened the strings.

I looked around to be sure nobody was watching me and moved toward the last building on the property. Completely bare of paint, this was the kind of weathered barn wood that some decorators love to use in their "shabby chic" remodels. Not my taste at all. I like clean and pristine. Old might be charming, but I'll take new any day.

Overgrown buckthorn and blackberry brambles tugged at my jacket as I crept around the corner of the barn toward the access door on the side.

I looked down. Boot prints. Three sets of boot prints leading across the field from the casino to this door.

Large boot prints flanked a set of slightly smaller ones. The larger treads were clear. Likely two men. The center prints showed walking, then stumbling, then walking again.

As I counted footprints, I pictured myself laying an ear to the ground like scouts do on old Westerns, announcing to the search party something like, "Ten horses, three days ride."

Of course, this was real life. No search party. Only me. And my cousin, needing my help.

I guessed that Krissy had been escorted, stumbling, maybe struggling, to this building by two men. Slade and Jacko, maybe?

I paused, thinking. *You don't know until you know.* I could be completely wrong. Maybe two guys and a girl, maybe all drunk, came out to this barn to mess around.

Maybe this had nothing to do with Krissy.

Then I saw it. Half-buried in the snow, a piece of golden metal with a glinting green eye. Part of Krissy's snake bracelet. I picked it up and slipped it on my left wrist.

Had it just fallen off in a fight? I hoped not. I hoped she'd dropped it on purpose, leaving a trail. A trail for me. On a previous case, I'd followed a paint trail to save a friend. Like Hansel and Gretel's breadcrumbs. *Good rule in life: Try to leave a trail.*

Krissy had been in this building, I was sure. Was she still inside? Alive? *Please God, yes? If anything happens to her, I'll never forgive myself. I am my cousin's keeper.*

The final question, if she was inside: Who else might be in there?

Badass knew there was only one way to find out. *We're going in.*

I pressed my ear against the wood of the door.

Silence.

I took a chance and slowly opened the door, just enough to slip through before pulling it shut behind me.

The smell of old hay and years of neglect hit me. I stifled a sneeze. I heard scurrying across the floor. I'd disturbed some rodent. Or maybe a bunch of them. *Ugh.*

As my eyes adjusted to the dark, I could make out the outlines of stalls to the left and right. I put my left hand on the top of the stall wall and inched my way forward. After several steps, I stopped, straining to listen.

More silence.

I took a risk and turned on my flashlight. The beam seemed doubly bright as it split the darkness of the barn. I jumped as a cat yowled in protest. It stood, back arched, blocking my path. It was missing an ear, and one eye bulged. Two more cats in similarly tough shape appeared behind it.

"Sorry, kitties," I whispered. I thought of Chloe. She was semi-feral and then adopted me after my apartment fire. Now she lives the life of Pampered Princess Kitty. These were mongrels from the back alley, or in this case, the back barn. I stamped my foot and hissed, "Shoo!" They scattered.

I waved the beam across the floor and through the space to the left and right. The light illuminated several stalls for long-gone horses, moldy hay, buckets, and old tack hanging on hooks. Several shovels and pitchforks were propped against the walls. The hay loft overhead had a rickety access ladder, covered in dust and cobwebs. Rectangular masses of old hay bales lined the edge of the loft.

I heard a sound. I turned off the flashlight and listened in the dark. Losing one sense heightens another. After a couple moments, I heard it again. A moan, coming from the far end of the barn.

Krissy.

I kept the flashlight beam tight to the floor as I crept quietly and quickly toward the sound. In an open stall at the end of the barn. Kris lay curled on her side, in a fetal position, partially covered with a filthy old horse blanket. Her hands were tied with rope behind her back, and that rope was tied to a post.

Her left foot was bare. Her boot and a pink sock lay on the floor next to her, and her ankle had a padlocked metal cuff around it. A shackle, like what you see on the ankles of prisoners in a dungeon, with a length of chain padlocked to the post.

I knelt beside her. "Krissy! It's me, Mack! Can you hear me?"

She moaned again. I felt her neck. Her pulse was weak but steady. I pulled the dirty blanket off her and swept the flashlight beam down her body. I saw no obvious signs of wounds. No blood. No bones. No joints askew.

Both of her eyes were swollen nearly shut. Her cheeks were starting to purple. Dried blood crusted from a cut by her mouth and another near her ear.

Someone had pummeled her face mercilessly. Maybe the same thugs who beat Jared.

A wave of fury coursed through me. "Hey, Kris, c'mon! Wake up!" I gave her shoulder a gentle shake. No response. I shook her harder. She moaned.

"I'd like to see the other guy," I joked, hoping to get a reaction. Nothing.

I tried to help her sit up. She muttered something that sounded like the F-word. Good sign. She forced her eyes to open, blinked several times, and licked her lips, mumbling, "Oh God, oh God."

"Krissy, it's me, Mack. Who did this? Was it Slade? Jacko? Marcus?"

She mumbled that swear word again, closed her eyes, and slumped back to the floor.

I had to get her out of the barn and to a doctor. I reached into my jeans pocket for my Swiss Army knife to cut the rope that held her to the post.

I heard a noise behind me. Before I could turn around, something hard slammed into the back of my head. I hit the floor and then nothing.

CHAPTER THIRTY-SIX

As I came to, Anxious whispered, *We really have to stop getting knocked out. And getting pushed in front of trains. And . . .* I took a breath to stop her recitation of "The List of Bad Things That Have Happened to Us."

I opened my eyes. Marcus Grubb was sitting on the hay bale in front of me, smoking a cigarette, with a shovel propped beside him. My cell and my flashlight lay on the floor next to him.

I sat up and rubbed the lump where that shovel had met my skull. I was on the floor next to Krissy, who was still breathing, thank God. I was tethered me to a post with a rope around my left wrist. Grubb hadn't bothered to restrain me any further.

I said, "Smoking is bad for your health, Mr. Grubb."

He gave a grunt. "So is snooping where you don't belong." He took a drag, then held up one of my TriMak cards. He'd obviously gone through my pockets, touched me while I was out. *Bastard. Slimy bastard.*

He exhaled smoke as he said, "So what are you doing here, uh, *Detective* Mackenzie Prentice?" A decidedly derisive tone there. "I guess you're not a cop after all, then, are you?"

"You got me there, Mr. Grubb." I learned to be polite early in life. And more recently, I've learned that it can make bad guys think you're soft. They relax, and then you have an advantage. Rational Me understands this, but Badass hates it when I'm polite to scumbags like Grubb.

He asked, "So why are you even here?" He pointed at Kris. "She's the only one this concerns."

I needed to keep him talking, to tell me things. Buying time while I figured out an escape plan. "Oh, I'm just her ride, that's all. Whatever she's done, that's on her." I shifted gears. "I have to say, Mr. Grubb, you've got quite an impressive operation here. You've done well for yourself. How did you even come up with this idea? It's pretty genius, I gotta say."

Bad guys love to brag when they figure you aren't going anywhere. Marcus Grubb was no exception. He finished his cigarette, took out another, and lit it off the tip of the first. He ground the first one into the floor by his feet. *Chain smoking. Definitely bad for the health. Die soon, slimy bastard.*

He smirked. "Damn right I've done well. Started with weekly poker games in my basement. Had a cover charge to pay for snacks and beer. I made a little money that way. So why not make more? Pretty soon, it was poker every night, then I put in a roulette wheel and charged twenty bucks to get in. Got too big for the basement, so I moved it to the barn." He gestured with his head toward the casino building. "Too bad you're stuck out here, or I'd give you a tour."

"I checked it out when I got here. Like I said, very impressive." I played dumb. "But I didn't realize this was tribal land."

He narrowed his eyes. "You know damn well it's not. But the local law knows to look the other way."

I wondered what kind of payoff Officer Anderson and the others were getting.

I said, "This is quite the enterprise to run all by yourself." Flattery. More pretending. Cards held tight to my vest.

He sucked on the cigarette, leveling a look at me before he said, "I've got partners."

I played a card. "From Chicago. The guys who paid Jared a visit." *Ooh, Mr. Grubb, wouldn't you like to know what else I know? About a federal investigation, maybe?*

He growled and ground the cigarette into the floor with the heel of his shoe. "Enough small talk."

"Just one more thing, Mr. Grubb," I said.

He snarled, "What's that?"

"I know where your money is. That's what you want, isn't it?"

He glared at me for a long time. He looked like it hurt to think so hard.

Those wheels are really rusty, Snarky said. I said, "I'll take you to it. Just let Krissy go, and I'll take you to the money.

"Ha! No way!"

I gave him a slow smile and played my next card. "I also have Clive Fenster's bones."

He stared at me, assessing.

I waited a few beats, then pressed on. "I'm pretty sure you want those back, don't you? Before the forensics guys figure out what happened. Pretty heavy penalty for murder one. And no statute of limitations."

He started to say something, then went mute.

Right on the money—or rather, the bones.

When he found his voice, he said, "What do you know about it?"

I served up another bluff. "I know you killed him, buried him, and let everybody think he'd just taken off. Nobody was any the wiser. You were home free. Why dig him up now?"

"You don't know shit! Enough screwin' around!" He stood and stepped toward Krissy. He reached down, grabbed her face, and yanked it toward himself. "Nobody steals from Marcus Grubb. Nobody!" He pressed his thumbs into her flesh. Her eyes went wide as she cried out.

I took deep breaths, trying to control my rising fury.

Grubb said, "She knows where the money is. I tried to get her to tell me, but she wouldn't." *Good Krissy. Brave Krissy.* "I left her in here to think about it, and I was just coming back to see if she'd changed her mind."

Krissy mumbled. "I don't—"

Grubb growled. "No lying little bitch is going to cheat me. Now, where is my damned money?" He squeezed harder. She gave a strangled cry.

I'd had enough. I yelled. "Leave her alone! She doesn't have your money! I've got it!"

He turned and glared at me.

I kept my voice level, authoritative. "Mr. Grubb, let her go. I've got the money, and I've got the bones. Let her go, and I'll take you to them. You'll have what you want, and I swear I won't tell anyone."

"Bull! You'll have to tell, even if you're not a cop!"

I stayed calm, spinning out a smooth lie. "Here's the thing, Mr. Grubb. I made a mistake letting you think I was a cop. I'm just a private investigator, and therefore, I have discretion about what I do after you let us go. And I can assure you I'll keep quiet. We have an ethical obligation to protect information and uphold the requirements of confidentiality."

"That's a lot of fancy words that all mean the same thing—bullshit!"

I raised my right hand. "No, Mr. Grubb, seriously. To be honest, I haven't exactly been playing by the rules in this investigation, and if I go to the authorities, I'll lose my license." Big fat lies, but he didn't need to know that. "So it's actually in my own best interest to keep my mouth shut. So how about it? I'll take you to your money and the bones. I have them both."

From his pained expression, he seemed to be thinking about it.

I resisted the urge to offer a pinky swear.

CHAPTER THIRTY-SEVEN

AFTER AN ETERNITY, MARCUS Grubb leveled a look at me. "You have my money. And the bones."

Aha! Maybe he does have something to do with Clive Fenster's death!

"Yes," I said. "I hid them, and I'll give them back. You take the money and the bones, and we walk away. Deal?"

He curled his lip. "Why should I make deals with a couple of stupid broads like you?"

"Think about it. I have your money. I have the bones. You kill us, and the *authorities* will have both. You deal with me, and *you* have both." I knew there wasn't a chance in hell that this guy would let us go once he had what he wanted. But I needed time to figure out how to get away from him.

He said nothing for a long moment, then gave a nasty chuckle. "Seems I got no choice."

I took that as agreement. I wriggled my left hand out of the rope around my wrist. I turned to Krissy. "Do you think you can walk?"

She nodded. "Just help me up."

I pointed to the shackle. "Where's the key for this?"

Grubb growled.

I yelled at him. "Hey! You want the money and the bones or not? Throw me the damn key!" I had the power now.

He swore, pulled a key from his pocket, and threw it toward me. I unlocked the padlock and removed the shackle, then put Krissy's sock and boot back on. The ankle was swollen, so I didn't lace the boot tightly.

I stood and helped Krissy to her feet. "You sure you can walk?"

She hobbled a few steps forward, regaining her balance. "Let's get out of here," she whispered.

Marcus was behind us, carrying the shovel. "Where's my money?"

"I'll take you there. You can follow us."

"Oh no." He grabbed Krissy by the arm. "I'll take her with me just so you don't try anything. You try anything, and you won't see her again."

Snarky snarked, *Try anything, and the dame gets it? Seriously?*

I said, "What? You're going to bury another body? Don't you have enough to worry about already?"

He snapped, "Shaddup! Get going!" He pushed Kris forward. She stumbled, and while he was distracted, I turned quickly and picked up my flashlight and my cell from the floor. I tucked the flashlight under my sweatshirt, and my phone into my sweatshirt pocket.

We walked Krissy to Grubb's car, which was parked behind the casino. I buckled her in the passenger's seat and whispered, "Watch for my signal." That's all I could say before Grubb got in behind the wheel.

Krissy said, dripping sarcasm, "Be sure to buckle up, Marcus."

As I walked to Cricket, I heard him yell at Kris to behave herself. *He has no idea who he's talking to*, Snarky said.

I headed out of the barnyard with Grubb following, and as I drove down the highway, Anxious Me freaked out. *What are we doing? We don't have the bones or the money! He's going to realize that. And we can't just drive to the cops. He'll take off and he has Krissy.*

Badass had a suggestion. *Now would be a great time to get a flat tire.*

A plan formed. I slowed way down, as if Cricket had an engine problem. I pulled to the side of the road and stopped. I popped the hood open, got out, and looked at the engine.

Grubb stopped his car and ran up to me, angry. "What the hell is going on?"

I kept my voice calm. "My car isn't working right. I've had this problem before. Just need to get my tools from the back, and I can fix it." I wanted to get the tire iron from the back of Cricket, but the snowplow truck had eliminated that possibility. But thanks to my anxious mother, in addition to BOB, the emergency suitcase, I also carry a canvas bag of emergency tools behind the driver's seat. *Just in case.*

I opened the back driver's-side door and dug through the tools in the canvas bag, feeling for the right one to use against Grubb. Hammer? No. Too puncture-y. Screwdriver? No. Too stabby. My fingers brushed against the flashlight under my shirt. Yes. Just right. *This will do nicely*, Badass opined.

"Hurry up! Ain't got all day!" Marcus didn't notice as I held the flashlight against my chest, both hands wrapped around it.

He also didn't notice Krissy sliding into the driver's seat of his car. He did, however, notice the squeal of tires as she threw it into reverse and floored it.

Grubb shouted, "What the f—k?" and turned to run for his car. His forward momentum stopped abruptly as I brought the flashlight down hard on his head.

The "great persuader" persuaded him to hit the pavement. He complied.

He really had no choice.

Krissy shifted into drive and came forward, fast. For a second, I thought she might just finish him off with his own car, but she stopped with one front tire resting very close to the guy's head.

She jumped out and hobbled to Cricket's passenger door, holding her right side. She yelled to me, "Let's get the hell out of here before he wakes up!"

I slammed Cricket's back door and got into the driver's seat. "Hope he doesn't decide to follow us," I said.

Krissy gave a laugh. "He'd need these!" She jangled Grubb's keys. Then she groaned, pressing a palm into her side. "I think that son of a bitch broke my ribs."

As I drove away, I looked in the rearview to see Marcus sit up on the pavement, rubbing the back of his head, and no doubt wondering how two "stupid broads" had gotten the better of him.

CHAPTER THIRTY-EIGHT

KRIS ASKED, "WHERE TO now, cuz?" I glanced at her. Hunks of straw clung to her hair. The old man pants and shirt were even more filthy than when the chief had given them to her. She had a black eye and welts purpling on both sides of her face. She pressed her hands against her right side.

I said, "We're going to the hospital to get you checked out."

She said, "No, no! We can do that later! I'm fine!" She handed me Grubb's keys. "Let's go back to the casino and see what these keys will open."

Badass admired her spunk. "You feel up to it?"

She said, "Hell yeah!"

I know how it can be when the adrenaline is flowing. "Hang on!" I hit the accelerator, and Cricket took off like a champ.

While we drove to the casino, Krissy used the visor mirror to pick the straw out of her hair. She lifted the bottom edge of the old man shirt, spit on it, and scrubbed the dried blood from her face.

She still looked like crap.

We got to the casino. Mr. Security was nowhere in sight. We headed for the cashier's booth. Charlene was on duty. She looked up at me through the glass partition. "Can I help you?" Her tone held impatience.

Krissy limped up next to me. Charlene saw her and shock registered. "Kris? Oh my God! What happened to you?"

In the harsh glare of the fluorescent casino lights, she looked even worse than she had outside. "Marcus happened to me."

Charlene went pale and pointed to the door on her right. "Come in here! Get off the casino floor." She unlocked the side door, we went in, and she locked the booth again behind us.

"Tell me," she said.

Krissy looked at me for permission. I'd made one of those instant judgments based on Charlene's reaction to Krissy's injuries. I nodded and said, "I think we can trust Charlene to help us."

Krissy filled her in. Charlene was appalled. "That bastard! That fat, effing bastard!" Her face flushed hot, and her hands balled into fists.

I said, "I think there may be evidence in his office that the authorities would be thrilled to have. Can you help us out?" I jingled the key ring. As empathetic as Charlene had been toward her friend, would she be willing to turn on her boss?

She was. She said, "I might have been reluctant before—this is my job, after all—but after what happened to Jared, and now seeing you, Kris, I say we nail the bastard!"

Determination in her step, she took the keys and unlocked her boss's office, flicking on the light switch as we followed her inside.

I looked around the space. A typical office layout—desk, chair, and a couple of filing cabinets. Papers stacked randomly on every surface. "Where would he conceal, uh, sensitive materials?"

Charlene's eyes slitted. "I know exactly where." She moved to a door at the back of the office, fiddled with the keys and unlocked it.

We entered a smaller room with piles of cardboard boxes stacked on the floor. I lifted a lid. Papers. The next box held poker chips and playing cards. The next, more papers. I said, "Not likely he'd leave incriminating evidence out in the open. Is there a safe somewhere?"

"Wait," she said, and started shifting boxes away from the center of the small room, uncovering a trap door in the floor, with a ring attached to lift it up. She looked at me. "I saw him in here one day. I don't know what's down there."

"Let's just take a look, shall we?" I tugged the ring and the wooden panel hinged upward.

Inside was a metal strongbox, maybe two feet square with a metal handle on the top. I pulled sleeves over my hands and lifted the box out. On Grubb's key ring, I found the key that fit the small padlock. As I inserted the key, I looked up. Krissy and Charlene hovered over me, their faces bright with eager anticipation.

"A little room, please, ladies?" They stepped back. I opened the strongbox.

Money. Lots of money. Twenty-dollar bills, wrapped in paper bands like they'd come from the bank. I didn't touch, but I looked closer. "I'm no expert, but I'm going to guess these will turn out to be counterfeit."

Tucked in next to the money was a red book. A ledger. Careful not to leave prints, I lifted the book out of the box and laid it open on top of the money. "Well, lookee here. Dates and dollars and initials. A record of the funny money transactions with, I'm going to guess, Grubb's mob connections. The feds will be thrilled to have this."

I put the ledger back and was about to close the box when something at the bottom of the box caught my eye. I picked it up.

A ring. A man's ring with a giant ruby in the center. I was pretty sure this was the ring Marietta French had described. The ring Clive Fenster wore—showing off with his ring and gold chains. "Look at this," I said, and Krissy and Charlene leaned in again. "The authorities will be very interested to hear Mr. Grubb's explanation for how a dead man's ruby ring ended up in his possession."

I snapped photos of everything, put it all back, locked the box, and closed the trap door, careful not to leave fingerprints. I took out my cell and called Agent Sterling. He asked me to text the pictures, and I did. I told him where he could find Marcus—out there on the highway with a bad headache. Sterling thanked me and said he and his crew would handle things moving forward. No need for me to stick around.

I turned to Charlene. "I have to get Krissy to the hospital. Federal agents will be here in five minutes. Don't let anyone else near this room." I remembered Mr. Muscles. "Where's the security guy I saw here earlier?"

She said, "Oh, that's Deke. He'll be gone for hours. His usual afternoon-er with one of the girls who works the night shift here." She frowned. "But what if Marcus comes back?"

I shook my head. "Marcus is stranded out there with no car keys." I glanced around the office. A baseball bat was leaning against a file cabinet. I handed it to Charlene. "If he somehow gets here before the feds and gives you any trouble, use this."

She smiled, took the bat, and swung it expertly.

"Impressive," I said.

She grinned. "Girls' state softball champs my senior year."

I wouldn't want to be Marcus on the receiving end of Charlene's swing.

Krissy gave a groan and pressed her side again. "Mack, it's getting hard to breathe."

"Hold on. We'll get you some help," I said and turned to Charlene. "You got this?"

Charlene gave me a salute. "Yes, ma'am!" She stepped to Krissy and took her hand. "I'm so sorry he did this to you. And I'm sorry I told Marcus that Delroy swapped cars with you. If I'd just kept my mouth shut!" She bit her lip. "Can you ever forgive me?" She had tears in her eyes.

Krissy went on, "We all make mistakes. I'll forgive you if you forgive me for fixing you up with that doofus—what was his name? Clem something?"

"Oh God! I'd forgotten about Clem!" They laughed together, friends reconciled.

"We've gotta go." We left Charlene, bat in hand, waiting for the feds. For Marcus's sake, I hoped the feds got there before he did.

As we walked out to Cricket, an official-looking black car pulled up to the casino door. Four men in black got out. I recognized Agent Sterling among them, but I couldn't stop to chat.

I drove as fast as I dared back to Our Lady of Mercy's ER in Three Rivers, hoping Krissy wouldn't die of internal bleeding before we got there. I needn't have worried. Two of the cuts on Krissy's face needed stitches, and the skin on her ankle had been rubbed raw by the shackle. The emergency room doctor warned her that she'd probably have issues with the tendons in her ankle for a while.

She told him how she'd sprained both ankles several times playing basketball in high school. "No sweat, doc. I'm used to my ankles making me miserable."

He smiled. "With the ankle, it's RICE. Rest, ice, compression, and elevation."

She gave him a thumbs-up. "I know the drill. I RICE'd my way through my basketball and running days."

I waited in the ER cubicle while they took Krissy for X-rays. My cell dinged with a text from Heather:

sorry car trouble cant come

Oh geez, we forgot about Heather. She would've been so PO'ed if she'd made the trip to Lost Creek for nothing. Badass whispered, *Who needs backup? We got 'er done!* I texted back:

no need / all is well but u still owe me one

She sent a thumbs-up.

Krissy's X-rays revealed no broken ribs. The doctor concluded she was just badly bruised. "Acetaminophen and ibuprofen as needed. Do you think you need anything stronger for the pain? Temporarily?"

Kris shook her head. "No way, Doc. I don't want any of that stuff, and I sure don't want it around my mother. She's got addictions up the wazoo. The last thing she needs is to add pain pills to the mix. No thanks."

The doctor smiled. "Good plan." He left. The nurse came in with Krissy's discharge instructions and then insisted on wheeling her out of the clinic in a wheelchair. Krissy didn't have the energy to protest.

I pulled Cricket to the portico outside the clinic doors. Krissy looked like she was half asleep in the wheelchair. Once we were heading to Fiona's, I told her how sorry I was that she'd been beaten up, sorry about her bruises, and her ankle. Sorry I hadn't been there to protect her.

She gave a sardonic laugh. "No sweat, cuz. When your whole life has been crap, what's a little more added to the pile?"

Badass was impressed with Krissy's toughness. The rest of me was also impressed.

And a little sad too.

CHAPTER THIRTY-NINE

I NOTICED THE CAMPER WAS gone from Fiona's driveway when I parked behind her house. She met us at the kitchen door. By the time I brought Kris the bottle of Extra-Strength Tylenol from the bathroom cabinet and a glass of water, Krissy was sound asleep.

Fiona was at the kitchen table, drinking a can of Sprite, deep lines of concern etched on her face. She'd been crying.

"She's going to be okay, Aunt Fiona. Don't worry."

She looked up at me, eyes red-rimmed and face puffy. "It's all my fault."

"No, it's not." I filled her in on what had happened at the casino—surface level, not the gory details. "You're not responsible for any of this."

"Oh, yes, I am. If I hadn't called Kristen to come home, if I hadn't pretended people were after me, if I weren't so damned pathetic—"

I held up a hand. "Wait. What?"

She looked down at the soda can and shook her head.

"There was a dead robin, but it was out in the yard." She looked toward the kitchen window. "And there were phone calls, but they never said anything. They were probably just wrong numbers. Or those stupid telemarketing calls."

"What about the crow?"

"I must have imagined all that." She looked at me. "It's happened before, you know? I have quite the imagination sometimes."

Ah yes. Fiona's "spells." "But what about the bird crap on your bedroom drape. I saw it."

"It was dry, wasn't it? It was paint, from painting the bedroom years ago."

I didn't say what I was thinking—that nobody should paint their bedroom the color of crow crap. "What about the noose?"

Fiona looked at the table. "There was no noose. I made that up, too."

I pushed away a surge of anger, trying to keep my voice calm. "Fiona, we did a stakeout. There was a person in the yard. They ran off."

Fiona said, "The morning after that, Mrs. McGruder stomped over here accusing me of trying to steal her chickens. She waved a note in my face. A note from somebody claiming to be from the Chicken Liberation Coalition, or something like that. Demanding that chickens shouldn't be cooped up, but that they should all be free-range."

So it was the would-be chicken liberator I'd tried to tackle that night.

Fiona said, "Estelle—that's Mrs. McGruder's name—accused me, but it turned out it was that granddaughter of hers, Pansy."

"You mean Marigold?"

"Oh yeah. I knew it was a flower. Yes. Sweet little Marigold. Her very own precious granddaughter planned to cut the fence and set the chickens free."

Sweet little Marigold probably had a pair of wire cutters in that sack she was carrying, and that's what jabbed me in the stomach. *Sweet little girl, my fanny.*

Fiona went on. "I told Estelle when she came back to apologize that the only thing I care about, as far as chickens are concerned, is whether they're fried or baked. She agreed that they're delicious, and we had a good laugh about that." Fiona chuckled. "She took me over there and introduced me to the chickens. It's hilarious, the names they have. Judy Garland? Lucille Ball? Cleopatra? Now that I *know* them, I promised Estelle that I'd help keep an eye on them. And she said she'd keep me supplied with eggs in return." Fiona frowned. "I don't know what that Marigold was thinking, setting those chickens free to be eaten by feral cats or the dogs. I wouldn't wish that on any creature—not even a chicken."

I leaned back and crossed my arms. "Speaking of dogs, I assume the Rottweilers next door were innocent as well?"

She gave a sheepish look. "Yes, there was dog poop on the sidewalk, not on my porch. I don't think they did that on purpose. They're actually very nice dogs."

Snarky muttered, *Unless they are fighting over a femur.*

Mr. Rooney hadn't responded to the note I left. "Would you please let Mr. Rooney know I don't need to talk to him anymore? That everything's been resolved?"

Fiona said she'd be glad to do that, maybe a little too eagerly. I suspected a spark there.

My aunt and her neighbors had reached a peaceful coexistence. "You made all that stuff up just to get Krissy to come home and help you?"

She nodded. "I'm not proud of what I've done. Before I called Kristen, I'd already decided to kick Harold out. I never should have taken him in, you know? He annoyed me from the start. Acting like an adolescent. And then he started making remarks about my collections. He even called me a hoarder once. Can you imagine?"

I bit my lip. All I could say was, "Wow."

"I know! The nerve! That was the last time he stayed in the house. He found that camper on Facebook Marketplace and moved it into the backyard. But the neighbors complained because it was so ugly. The police came, and the one officer said there was no law against ugly, but there is a law against living in a camper in the city. So, we pretended Harold was just storing the camper in the yard. He used a flashlight when he was sleeping out there, so the neighbors didn't suspect."

She took a glug of her Sprite, then went on. "The final straw was that marriage business—that thing he was supposedly doing online."

I said, "Oh yeah. I did some research. That kind of thing is perfectly legal as long as all parties are adults and aware of the deal."

Fiona scowled. "It might be legal, but with Harold it was just a big lie. He was actually connecting with all those women himself. Lying to them!"

"So there was no dissatisfied customer?"

"No, that guy was just somebody Harold owed money to. Anyway, I snuck a look at his computer a couple weeks ago and figured out it was all a scam. I was just waiting, giving him enough rope to hang himself. Then yesterday, one of those women showed up at the door, said she was looking for her fiancé. Meaning Harold! Can you imagine that? I hollered for him to come into the house. He saw her and confessed. That was it. I told him to get his sorry ass and his ugly camper off my property. The two of them drove off together." She shook her head. "Geez, I sure know how to pick 'em, don't I?"

I shrugged. "Don't beat yourself up. I've certainly put up with nonsense in relationships, just to avoid being alone."

Fiona nodded. "That's my problem. I don't want to be alone. I thought if Kristen came home, we could start over. She's my daughter, and I love her, and I know I've got some things in the past to make up for. I hope she'll forgive me." She focused on the Sprite. "Maybe she'll stay with me. She's single. I'm single. Just us two girls . . ." She trailed off, biting her lower lip.

I patted Fiona's hand. "I'm guessing Krissy will stay for a little while. She told me she'd like to help you clean up around here." Not exactly what Krissy said. What she'd said involved a lot of swear words, but I knew my cousin had a strong desire to see her mother's mess cleaned up.

Fiona looked surprised. "She said that? That would be wonderful. I just feel like everything has gotten away from me."

I hesitated to broach the subject, but then I went for it. "What about your drinking? I know that really bothers Kris." I didn't mention that it bothered the rest of the family too. Fiona had heard that plenty of times before.

She grinned. "Oh, absolutely! If she agrees to stay, I'll quit. I'll go to AA tomorrow!" She gave a sigh. "All I want is a fresh start. For both of us." She waved a hand around the room. "I'm done with all this nonsense."

I knew firsthand about trying to fill some kind of emptiness with alcohol, sugar, or other things. Now that I wasn't drinking anymore, I'd had time to think about why I drank. Anxiety. Fear of abandonment. Trying to fix those feelings with alcohol was like trying to fix a broken leg with a Band-Aid. Completely hopeless and a huge waste of energy.

I thought Fiona might need a little more help than just the local AA meetings. Maybe she'd see a therapist. Or maybe a stint in rehab was needed. But that was a conversation for another time. *Baby steps, baby steps.*

Fiona walked with me to check on Krissy, who was sleeping soundly on the couch.

I said, quietly so as not to wake Kris, "Aunt Fiona, one great place to start would be for you to get her room cleaned up. She's going to need a place to sleep while she's recovering from all this."

Fiona's face brightened. "I'll do that! I'll start right now. See yourself out, won't you?" She took off up the stairs to Krissy's bedroom.

Krissy didn't open her eyes, but she gave a little smile. "Thanks, Dork."

I bent down, kissed my cousin on the forehead, and whispered, "You're welcome."

CHAPTER FORTY

Thursday, November 27, Thanksgiving Day

I'D TEXTED CHIEF BRONSON before I went to bed the previous night. I told him I had something I needed to give to Agent Sterling. The chief texted me early on Thanksgiving morning, asking me to meet him at the office. I stopped by Gram's and told her I'd come back later to help peel potatoes, then headed to TriMak.

Agent Sterling was waiting in the chief's office. His black sweatshirt had the Secret Service logo on the upper right.

I handed him the Longacre Feed and Seed sack with what was left of Krissy's casino winnings. "What's going to happen to my cousin? And my aunt? They had no idea any of this was counterfeit. And my cousin didn't know it wasn't okay to spend the money she won at the illegal casino. As soon as I told her, she stopped spending it."

"We'll want to interview them both, but if what you say is true, there's no intent to defraud. Receiving counterfeit currency without knowing it makes you a victim, not a criminal."

I felt a wave of relief.

Sterling filled us in on the case as events had unfolded so far. Marcus Grubb was in custody. The federal agents had taken the stuff from the floor of his office. "Valuable information. Filled in some very big blanks in the case. Mr. Grubb, as expected, denied knowing anything about the counterfeit currency that his mob friends were filtering through his gambling operation. Their network includes other businesses in the six surrounding states, as well." According to Agent Sterling, nobody was buying Grubb's protestations of innocence, and he faced federal racketeering charges for possessing and distributing counterfeit currency, and likely tax evasion. "Of course, he can help himself if he chooses to cooperate with us to bring down bigger fish."

The chief added, "And the state will want to nail him for running an illegal casino, so that's extra leverage to persuade him to cooperate."

I asked, "That casino was there for a long time. I assume the local cops were paid to ignore it?"

Agent Sterling said, "Maybe in the past, but Officer Anderson and his team have been instrumental in bringing this case together. They'll all be testifying."

"What about the bones we found? Did Grubb kill him? Will there be a murder charge against Grubb?"

Agent Sterling nodded to the chief. "You want to take this?"

The chief spoke. "He copped to burying the body, but said it was his aunt who actually killed Clive Fenster. The owner of that red truck you asked about."

My jaw dropped. Puzzle pieces clicked into place in my real-life game of Clue. "Marietta French. Marcus Grubb is her nephew." Marietta French, owner of the red truck, driven by her nephew's minions, Slade and Jacko, stealing from Krissy, following us. Marietta French with the black truck with the snowplow, trying to kill me with a train.

I told the chief and Sterling about the incident at the railroad tracks. "I reported it to Lakeland County."

The chief said, "It's a hit and run, Mack. Not your fault. Not to worry. You reported it. That's all you're required to do. The railroad takes it from there."

"I figured as much, Chief. But I will let them know who was driving the black truck with the plow. I understand now why Marietta French wanted to shut me up. She didn't want me digging into Fenster's death. She killed him. I'd never have guessed."

The chief nodded. "Yes. According to Grubb, his aunt told him Fenster said he'd make her money troubles go away in exchange for sex. When she refused, he tried to rape her. She hit him with a shovel."

That family's weapon of choice. I was lucky I didn't end up a bag of bones after Marcus Grubb used a shovel to knock me out in the barn.

The chief said, "She's likely to plead self-defense. But Grubb buried the body for her, so he'll be charged with concealing a corpse, at least."

"I don't understand why he dug the body up. He was home free."

Chief Bonson nodded. "Yes, he would have been, but construction had started on a new development on that land, and he knew it wouldn't be long before the body was discovered. He stashed the bag in the old car, never expecting it to end up with your cousin."

I turned to Agent Sterling. "French is connected to the casino too, I think. In business with her nephew, I'd guess. I saw her carrying a duffel bag out of there." *Another click. Slade and Jacko had a duffel bag, according to that motel clerk in Three Rivers. Same one? Perhaps.*

"Interesting," Sterling said. "Just let me send a quick text to my team to track that down." He tapped the phone, then smiled at me. "Good information, Detective. Thanks."

I smiled back, then turned to the chief. "What's going to happen to Fenster's bones now? It seems he has no family."

The chief said, "The M.E. will hold the remains for a time, waiting to see if someone will claim them."

I felt bad that any person, no matter who they were or what they'd done, would be left unclaimed. I also knew that Clive Fenster, for all his misdeeds, had helped at least *some* people in Lost Creek. People are never all bad, or all good.

Agent Sterling said, "Thanks to the evidence you found, Detective Prentice, the casino is shut down, and we expect those who worked there to cooperate with our efforts. Otherwise, they'll face charges of their own. The consequences can be stiff."

I was confident that Jared Clark and Charlene Bean would be happy to do what they could to make sure Marcus Grubb got what he deserved. "What about Grubb's two other cronies? They called themselves Slade and Jacko. No clue about last names."

Sterling shrugged. "This is the first I've heard of them."

"Minor players," I said. "They probably took off as soon as things started going south for Grubb. But they likely have counterfeit money in their possession." I didn't mention it had come from Krissy's stash. "Last time I saw them, they were driving that red truck owned by Marietta French." I texted him the picture of the plate.

He looked at his cell, then sent another text to his team. "Thanks. That's most helpful. We'll find them." He paused and shot me a tight smile. "We always do."

He pocketed his phone. "Meanwhile, Grubb will be going to prison. For how long will depend on his willingness to provide information about his, uh, friends."

The chief looked serious. "Mack, you may be called to testify as well."

I felt a little tremor in my stomach. As if it were the 1920s and testifying would put me on Al Capone's hit list. Or the godfather would be making me an offer I couldn't refuse. Anxious Me was certain that testifying was a very, very bad idea.

Badass Me overruled her. "Happy to do my duty," I said and gave Agent Sterling a little salute.

He gave a quick nod. "Glad to hear it. Now I'll be off." He stood and put on his long, black coat. "Thank you for your cooperation, both of you." He walked toward the office door, then turned and smiled, warmth lighting his eyes. Attractive, that warmth. "And a happy Thanksgiving."

After Agent Sterling was gone, I looked at the chief. He was grinning. Big.

"What are you smiling about?"

"Chickie, Chickie, Chickie. I have to say, from what Sterling told me about how everything came together—you finding the evidence, saving your cousin—you are one tough investigator. Tough. Tenacious. Smart." He stood. "All I can say is well done, Chickie. Well done." He reached out and shook my hand, then put his left hand over the top of mine and squeezed. "Well done."

We closed up the office for the four-day weekend. The chief left for another deer hunting trip with his friend, Judge Carson.

And I—Tough, Tenacious, Smart, Impressive Badass Detective Mackenzie Prentice—headed to Gram's.

Those Thanksgiving potatoes weren't going to peel themselves.

CHAPTER FORTY-ONE

BY TWO THAT AFTERNOON, the potatoes were cooked and mashed, the turkey stuffed and baked. The side dishes—sweet potatoes, scalloped corn, cranberries, and the rest sat ready as we all gathered around Gram's big dining room table. On the sideboard, pumpkin pie, a cherry-topped cream cheese dessert, a platter of cookies, and Gram's homemade fudge waited.

Gram's house smelled the way it always smells on Thanksgiving Day—like home. Like love.

The Thanksgiving crowd this year included Gram and Nathan, brother Greg, his wife, Sarah, and their three kids. My little sister, Deanne, was there, too, with her husband and their four children.

Big sister Stephanie was alone at the table. She and her consort, a wealthy older man named Mason, were on the outs at the moment. She was pretending not to care about that.

The only sibling missing was my younger brother, Robbie. He was in Amsterdam, on the movie set for an adaptation of his latest novel. He writes spy thrillers. Not my kind of reading, but his books are incredibly popular among a certain demographic.

Fiona came sans Harold, who was off to parts unknown with his internet "fiancée." And Krissy was there, bandaged and bruised, but not broken.

I sat back, watching everyone. A full house. Just the way Gram likes it. I like it too.

Six grandchildren—Greg's three and three of Deanne's—sat at the kids' table in the front parlor, easily visible to their parents through the Victorian's open pocket doors.

Nine adults in the dining room. Deanne held her baby, six-month-old Tulip, in her arms at the table. I marveled at Deanne's ability to eat one-handed.

The baby's official name is Nadine, after Deanne's husband's grandmother, but we call her Tulip because of the way she sticks out her little lips when she's sleeping. I've seen it, and I have to say, it is pretty darn adorable.

I smiled. *This is my happy place, surrounded by my big, crazy family. No place on earth I'd rather be.*

Midway through the meal, Fiona stood and tapped her butter knife against her water glass. "I have an announcement."

We all got quiet.

She said, "First of all, I want to thank Mackenzie for her help."

I tried to look humble. *Just doing my job, ma'am. Just doing my job.*

Fiona went on. "And I want to thank Kristen for coming to my rescue."

Krissy grinned at her mother, looking pleased with herself. Fiona bent and kissed her on the cheek.

Fiona looked at me and said, "I called that E-Z MONEY lady—Laureen—and she's coming over on Monday to set up a payment plan for me. I'll be able to get my car back, I hope."

Sister Stephanie perked up. "Fiona, I might be able to help you out. We can talk later."

Fiona thanked her, and then said to the family, "You'll all be happy to hear that I kicked Harold to the curb. He was a lying rat."

Gram blurted, "Praise the Lord!"

"And one last thing," Fiona said. "I need to downsize. Kristen has agreed to stay and help me. Then maybe I'll sell the house and find a smaller place." Fiona looked down at Krissy. "Did I cover everything?"

Kris whispered something to her. Fiona cleared her throat. "Oh yeah, the *last,* last thing. I've been sober for two days now, and I'm joining AA."

Everyone applauded then, and my mother and Gram both got up and hugged Fiona.

Fiona turned bright red. "Geez Louise, you're acting like I discovered the cure for cancer. It's just AA, for God's sake."

That brought a laugh around the table. The conversation continued, light and happy chatter for the rest of dinner.

After dinner, I sat on the family room couch with Deanne while she nursed Tulip. Deanne updated me on all that was going on in her world. Gram brought Deanne the soft, pink, crocheted blanket she'd made for Tulip. Deanne wrapped it around the baby, then stood and handed Tulip to me. "Hold her, will you? I've really gotta go." She walked fast toward the powder room.

I looked down into Tulip's little face. She stared at me. You know how a baby can stare at you, and look so wise, as if they understand how the whole world works? Tulip gave me one of those knowing looks, and then she smiled.

"Yes, Tulip," I cooed at her. "That's right, I'm your Auntie Mack. And we're going to have so much fun together. Yes, we are." I gurgled and cooed—just one of those goofy people who gurgle and coo at babies. I gurgled and cooed, and felt every tough, badass fiber of my being melting away into mush.

What is that about? I bent my head and sniffed Tulip's little head. Her fuzzy hair tickled my nose. She gave a little cough, and a curdle of what Deanne had just fed her dribbled out of her mouth. Instead of finding that sickening, I decided it was just part of her adorableness.

Snarky was disgusted. *You're going soft, Sherlock.*

Badass Me was a little concerned as well. *Don't get any ideas about having one of these yourself. You've got a career going, remember? You're Badass Detective Mackenzie Prentice.*

Rational Me told both of them to shut up. Plenty of mothers out there have a family and a career. It's easier for women today to be accepted for whatever choices they make. Not like when Gram and all the other moms were stay-at-home mothers. When I was a kid and my dad left us, my mother had to go to work. If not for Gram taking us in after school, we would have been "latchkey" kids, and that would have devolved quickly into some kind of *Lord of the Flies* situation.

Gram. Always there. Always here, for all of us.

Tulip gave a little sigh and fell asleep in my arms. *Maximum meltiness*, Lonely Me concluded. I held her little body against me. Warm. Soft. The picture of contentment and peace.

I had almost nodded off when Deanne came to retrieve the baby. "I'll put her upstairs. Nap time."

For a moment, I thought about refusing to give her up. I

wanted to tell Deanne to go find her own baby, which was ridiculous. Reluctantly, I surrendered Tulip. As I watched Deanne carry her away, my biological clock ticked so loudly I was sure everyone in the house could hear it.

MUCH LATER, AFTER DINNER AND DISHES, after pie and coffee, after the annual post-dinner family walk, I was alone in the kitchen, wiping off the counters. I heard a knock at Gram's back door.

I looked up. Nick was there, smiling at me through the window. I opened the door.

"Happy Thanksgiving, Mack," he said. "My family is all at my granddad's, but I snuck away to bring you these." He held out a bouquet of yellow and red alstroemeria, which has always been Gram's favorite flower, and now is my favorite as well. Gram reminds me that the name is pronounced, "I'll still marry ya."

"Beautiful," I said. I touched one of the blossoms. "My favorites."

"I know," he said softly.

I invited him to come in, but he declined. "I have to get back. I just wanted to see you."

I sighed. "Nick, the last time I saw you, you were with Bo Peep at Jimmy's Pizza."

He looked confused. "Who?"

"Hillary Sharp. I assumed you were dating her."

He shook his head. "Her? No, that was nothing. We met at Jimmy's, and if you'd stuck around, you'd have seen Spider. The three of us had pizza, and then I left."

Not the first time I'd jumped to an incorrect conclusion.

Nick cleared his throat and said, "I've been thinking about you. And our future."

Our future.

I heard the kids behind me, raucous, laughing, wild, chasing one another in an indoor game of tag. One of Deanne's let out a screech, followed by the thunder of kids' feet across Gram's hardwood floors.

Could I have wild, raucous children of my own in that future?

I looked into Nick's soft brown eyes. Sincere, reliable, dependable eyes. He drew me close. He smelled like Old Spice and clean sheets.

We could stay here in his arms forever.

His voice husky, he whispered, "So what do you think, Mackenzie?"

"About what?"

He pulled away, met my eyes. He *looked* at me. The way Gram had described somebody looking at you, as if they see something special. Something they like.

Nick hesitated, then smiled. Those dimples. "What do you think about the future? Us. Together." He pulled me close, and I felt the prickle of his breath as he whispered against my neck. "That's what I want. But I don't know what you want."

"Nick, I—"

He pulled away again, put his finger against my lips. "No, don't answer me right now. Don't give me an answer until you're sure." His eyes drilled into mine. "I want you to be sure. So, think about it, okay?"

With that, he kissed me, long and warm, then smiled and let me go.

I felt all melty as I watched him walk out to his Land Rover.

Think about it?

Oh, I'd think about it, yes.

Every part of me agreed—I'd be thinking of little else.

If Mackenzie Prentice and her inner committee made you smile, I'd be so grateful if you left a quick review. A sentence or two from you helps other readers discover the series and means more to me than you might imagine.

With deep gratitude,

Mary

COMING SOON: Book Seven in the series

MACK ON ICE

A Mackenzie Prentice Mystery

"I tripped and fell, face-first, unto the frozen lake.
I opened my eyes and looked down.
Someone stared up at me through the ice. Someone
very frozen. And very dead.
But that's not where this story starts."

IT'S WINTER IN THREE Rivers and a polar vortex has settled over the region, freezing the lakes and landscape weeks ahead of schedule. Despite the frigid weather, Mackenzie Prentice and the TriMak crew are heading for the annual ice fishing contest and winter celebration at Lake Keewaukee. While Mack is there, a woman begs her to find her brother—a renowned carver of much-in-demand wooden fishing decoys—who has vanished without a trace.

The frozen maze of this mystery stretches far beyond the festival, pulling Mack along a frostbitten trail of deceit, denial, and double-crosses. She's racing the clock and the cold. Will she be able to find her man in time? Or is it already too late?

Mackenzie Prentice, Investigator—thirty-five, a sugar addict with a touch of OCD and a chorus of voices in her head commenting on her choices—still has things to work out in her personal life. But on the job, she's tough, tenacious, and enough of a badass to handle whatever this winter throws at her—or so she hopes.

Author Mary Pierce shares her home in Wisconsin with her husband, Terry, and their goldendoodle, Sammy, named after their favorite pizza place. You can find Mary on Substack: *Old Woman, New Life by Mary Pierce* at marypierce.substack.com.

ACKNOWLEDGMENTS

THANKS TO YOU FIRST, DEAR READER, for spending some of your precious time in Three Rivers with Mackenzie and the gang. You keep reading, and I'll keep writing.

Thank you, Michelle Rayburn (missionandmedia.com) for cheerleading, editing, designing, and consulting. Your leadership and generosity in this indie publishing paradigm are amazing.

Thank you to Joe Coughlin for generously sharing his expertise in law enforcement. (Errors in that area are strictly my own.)

Thanks to the family clan. Alex, Katy, Liz, Jenny, Laura, Dan, partners, and children. So grateful to have you all.

Thanks to my fellow Substack writers who inspire me with their love of language and vulnerability. I draw inspiration—and courage—from all of you.

And to Aron Croft (hiddenadhd.com) and the PTA family, thank you for your support, coaching (Deb), and for all the study hall pals who help me stay focused: Ivy, Martha, Tammy, Renee, Ruth, Jayne, Annie, Caitie, Lucy, Katalin, the Sarahs, Carla, Heidi, Tim, Scott, Peter and the rest. Altogether now: "Consistency over intensity!"

To faithful early readers: Maureen, Dan, Kelly, Neenee, Janis, Melyssa, Fern, Laura, Paula, Mary Lee, Jane, Nancy, Joan, Rick, Liz, Jessie, Deirdre, Ashley, Barbara, and Mack's growing base of fans, thank you for your enthusiasm in spreading the word. I love you all!

Finally, thank you, my darling Terry, for four decades of love and encouragement. I'd be lost without you.

ABOUT THE AUTHOR

MARY PIERCE IS THE AUTHOR OF the Mackenzie Prentice Mysteries, a lifelong dream. She is also the author of three books of humorous inspiration / memoir published by Harper Collins/Zondervan: *When Did I Stop Being Barbie and Become Mrs. Potato Head*; *Confessions of a Prayer Wimp*; and *When Did My Life Become a Game of Twister*, along with hundreds of articles and a humor column for a national magazine.

Mary spent twenty years as a keynote humorist, bringing laughter and encouragement to audiences at women's wellness events and retreats around the country.

She left the speaking circuit to care for her aging mother, who had dementia. After six years as primary family caregiver, Mary returned to school, earning a master's degree in Clinical Mental Health Counseling at the age of sixty. As a licensed psychotherapist, she works with adults who are dealing with depression, anxiety, and life changes, specializing in trauma reprocessing and support for family caregivers.

Mary enjoys designing her book cover art, sketching, art journaling, and messing around with collage and assemblage as a mixed media artist. (Paint? Glue? Ripping paper? What's not to love?)

She and her husband, Terry, share six children and eleven grandchildren. They make their home in Wisconsin with Sammy, the goldendoodle. You can find Mary on Substack: *Old Woman, New Life by Mary Pierce* at **marypierce.substack.com**.

www.ingramcontent.com/pod-product-compliance
Lightning Source LLC
LaVergne TN
LVHW090559110826
845146LV00001B/190

* 9 7 9 8 9 8 8 1 7 7 6 1 6 *